W9-CEJ-500

MISTER BOOTS

BOOKS BY CAROL EMSHWILLER

NOVELS
Carmen Dog
Ledoyt
Leaping Man Hill
The Mount
Mister Boots

STORY COLLECTIONS
Joy in Our Cause
Verging on the Pertinent
The Start of the End of It All
Report to the Men's Club and Other Stories
I Live with You and You Don't Know It

CAROL EMSHWILLER

MISTER BOOTS

· a fantasy novel ·

VIKING

VIKING

Published by Penguin Group

Penguin Young Readers Group, 345 Hudson Street, New York, New York 10014, U.S.A.

Penguin Books Ltd, 80 Strand, London WC2R 0RL, England

Penguin Books Australia Ltd, 250 Camberwell Road, Camberwell, Victoria 3124, Australia

Penguin Books Canada Ltd, 10 Alcorn Avenue, Toronto, Ontario, Canada M4V 3B2

Penguin Group (NZ), cnr Airborne and Rosedale Roads, Albany, Auckland 1310, New Zealand

First published in 2005 by Viking, a division of Penguin Young Readers Group

1 3 5 7 9 10 8 6 4 2

Copyright © Carol Emshwiller, 2005

All rights reserved

LIBRARY OF CONGRESS CATALOGING-IN-PUBLICATION DATA

Emshwiller, Carol.

Mister Boots : a fantasy novel / Carol Emshwiller.

p. cm.

Summary: The life of ten-year-old Bobby Lassiter changes drastically
when she meets Mister Boots, a man who is also a horse.

ISBN 0-670-05968-4 (hardcover)

[1. Horses—Fiction. 2. Metamorphosis—Fiction.
3. Magic—Fiction. 4. Fathers—Fiction.] I. Title.

PZ7.E69627Mis 2005

[Fic]—dc22

2005003950

Printed in USA   Set in Garamond 3   Book design by Jim Hoover

Without limiting the rights under copyright reserved above, no part of this publication may be
reproduced, stored in or introduced into a retrieval system, or transmitted, in any form or by any
means (electronic, mechanical, photocopying, recording, or otherwise), without the prior written
permission of both the copyright owner and the above publisher of this book. The scanning,
uploading, and distribution of this book via the Internet or via any other means without the
permission of the publisher is illegal and punishable by law. Please purchase only authorized
electronic editions, and do not participate in or encourage electronic piracy of copyrighted
materials. Your support of the author's rights is appreciated.

To Eve, Susan, and Stoney

and to David

chapter one

I was born (which is a lucky thing in itself, and I'm lucky that I'm me and no one other). But also I'm lucky I was born right here, because I have the whole place to myself and nobody bothers me. Twenty-five acres of nothing—desert nothing—surrounded by other people's even bigger nothing. And I have the best mother because she doesn't care. I mean she loves me, but she doesn't care what I do. I can go out the window in the middle of the night. I can sleep under the stars. . . . And I'm lucky in having my big sister. She does all the things I'd have to do if she wasn't here. She likes to do everything I hate the most. And I'm lucky to have Mister Boots. Nobody knows about him but me.

My mother and my sister have too many of their own things to think about to worry about me. Like money. Like the next meal. Like new shoes. (I don't wear shoes, which is another lucky thing, but they do.)

Their minds are on their knitting. Their needles go wobbling back and forth all day. They make sweaters and caps and socks and lots of things for babies. They can't afford to make anything for themselves (or me). My old sweater barely comes down to my elbows. Mother keeps saying she should knit me another and what color do I want? I keep telling her sky blue, but does a sky blue sweater ever come along in my size?

Mother calls me Dear and Sweetie and Honey. My sister calls me Bobby and Booby. I wonder if anybody around here remembers my name? I've been called "cute" things all my life, and I never did like "cute," but I don't care, I have names I call myself to myself, like Scar.

And I do have scars crisscrossing my legs, but I don't remember how I got them. Maybe I was too little to keep away from a Spanish dagger plant. (Mister Boots has the exact same kinds of scars, and other bigger ones, too, where a whole chunk of skin came off.) I have a crooked elbow that won't go straight, but it doesn't bother me. My bad arm can do anything my good arm can do. I remember flying through the air once, but I don't know if I got thrown or dropped. Maybe I fell out of a tree. Or maybe I thought I could fly (I do remember thinking that now and then), and found out I couldn't.

They say my mother is past looking out for me or anybody and that's why I have these scars and such. (A baby needs somebody to pay attention.) They say our little graveyard just got too full up for her before I came . . . all her little boys died at birth. Bad for her, but lucky for me because I don't want any looking after. Besides, what could happen that wouldn't have already happened? Except Mister Boots happened. That's one new thing.

My sister is beautiful, but she's so shy. Boys from the nearest ranch hang around sometimes but not for long. She doesn't have time for them anyway; she has to help Mother with the knitting and everything else, and she's the one who has to take the knit things to the towns—to all the little stores. Mother won't go. I wouldn't mind going, but I won't help with the knitting. They know better than to ask me.

My sister has golden hair exactly the right length to hide behind. She shakes her head so her hair hangs down in front of her face and she peers out from behind it. She thinks she's safer back there. I suppose she is when she cries or when she blushes, which she always does. She says she hates herself when she cries. I never cry. I'd hate myself, too, if I did.

She has to go to all the little towns by hitchhiking. She hates that more than anything, but she has to do it. She always has a big suitcase full of knit things, and the circle she has to make is too far for walking. Even the closest village is four miles away. The whole loop she makes is almost too far even for the wagons she hitches rides with. I wouldn't mind hitchhiking, but they think I'm too young. I don't know why it's any safer for a beautiful girl to be doing it than me.

Once she even got a ride in a car. That really made me jealous. There are hardly any cars around, though they say pretty soon there'll be lots. (I can just imagine, *a-ooo-ga, a-ooo-ga* all over the place.) They're mostly owned by people not from here. Nobody's that rich even in our biggest town. That's eight miles from here. I've never even been there.

I'm the midnight moonlight starbright rider. We don't have any horses—we can't afford them—but the neighbors do. Their horses come to me all by themselves, no grain, no carrot, no apple. They follow me to the fence where I can get on, or I put them in an irrigation ditch and I get on from the bank.

Mister Boots says he'll never ever, ever ride a horse. Never! Even if his legs don't get well, he'll not ride, and that's that.

I almost made a big mistake. I told Mother that once a whirl-wind picked me up and put me down someplace else. I said, "I remember it," but Mother said, "Little and light as you are, that just couldn't happen." I told her Mister Boots said it could. I'm not even supposed to go to the next ranch over and talk to the wranglers, let alone to somebody like Boots.

"Mister Boots," she said. "What Mister Boots?"

And then I remembered she doesn't know about him and isn't supposed to.

"Nothing," I said. "Nobody and nothing."

She said, "Honey . . ." (How can you ever learn your real name if you're always called Honey or Sweetie Pie?) "I guess you haven't been homeschooled enough about reality and science. It's nice to make things up sometimes, but you have to stop believing whatever comes to mind. Mister Boots, for heaven's sake! What will you be thinking of next?"

So then I felt safe because she wouldn't believe in him anyway. But Boots isn't a name that's just out hanging on a tree—unless it's for a cat. Or, of course, a horse with four black feet.

How I found Mister Boots is, I was out in the middle of the night riding like I do, and I came to this naked man curled up under our one and only big tree, which is half dead because there hasn't been enough water lately. I always take bucketsful out there. Just then I had two canvas buckets, one on each side of the horse's withers, and I rode up and slid off, not knowing if I should give some to the man or all to the tree. I figured the man was as thirsty as the tree, and the tree as thirsty as the man, but the man was asleep, and besides, the tree is my friend.

But right then he woke up and started looking thirsty. So I gave him a drink. He said, "Thank you kindly," three times. "I'm grateful." After he'd had a drink, he patted the tree trunk as if he was as much friends with it as I am, and said, "It's thirsty, too," so I knew he was like me.

Then he looked down at himself as if he just realized he was naked. "You wouldn't happen to have clothes that might fit me a little bit?"

We did have some men's clothes packed away at home, so I said yes, and that I'd get them right now because it was a cool night.

Then he said, "Can you keep a secret?"

"Course I can."

"Can you keep me a secret?"

"Course." (It isn't as if I haven't kept almost everything a secret anyway. My whole life is a secret.) "Why? Are you a bank robber or what? Or maybe you escaped from someplace where they put crazies."

"I'm not. I didn't."

"Why should I believe you? Looks kind of funny, you out here naked and limping."

"Would a bank robber be naked?" He asked it as if he really wondered.

"Maybe your clothes were for prisoners. And maybe you hurt your legs jumping out a jail window."

"I don't have a weapon, not even a knife."

He couldn't be too bad, because he did know the tree was thirsty. "I do believe you."

I asked him how he lost his clothes, and he said, "I didn't have any," and I said, "If you didn't have clothes before, why do you need some now?" and he said, "It's your way, not mine," and I said, "Why?" Then he laughed, and said, "You don't know much more than I do," and I said, "I know just enough for right here and right now," and he laughed some more, and then I went and got him pants, and a nice warm shirt, and shoes and socks. . . . "The whole caboodle," he said, and then, "Isn't that a nice word?"

I guess I'd have to say I stole those clothes, but nobody was using them. I was hoping to get big enough to wear them myself pretty soon, but it takes a long, long time to grow even a little bit.

I never did dare ask Mother about the clothes. Why were they just hanging there for years and years in the spare room that never gets used for anything? Why didn't she give them to somebody? Or sell some? There's two silky shirts. I'll bet they're worth something. There's a dressy jacket with tails in back with pockets sewn inside them. There's even a purple turban with a jewel pinned on it.

I didn't bring Mister Boots any of those fancy things, I just brought ordinary clothes. At least now I know whoever they belonged to wasn't as tall as Boots and was chubby.

I've been looking after him for a couple of weeks now while his legs get better. Like he says himself, if not for me, he'd be naked and starving. "And worse than that, just plain dead."

He says, "Boy." (Just like everybody else, he doesn't

know what I really am. Nobody does, and if they once knew, they forget, even my mother! But I guess I can't fault her for that. Sometimes I forget it, myself.)

He never says, "What have you been up to?" like everybody else does, but I tell him anyway. I might tell things to my sister, but she's so wispy, and I don't think she approves of me. She thinks I should be more ladylike. Once she said, "I'd love to have a little sister who isn't so much like a little brother."

I tell Boots about how lucky I am and how magic, except nothing ever happens around here, but he looks at me like he doesn't think I'm as lucky as I think I am. He says, "Don't worry, what happens will come, and sometimes hardly any time between one thing and another. I was told that by an old man when I was young. Up there in the mountains." He gestures with his chin. "That man said, 'All in good time,' and he was right because it *is* all in good time, as look, I'm here right now."

"First of all, I don't worry, and second of all, nothing's gone on around here. To you maybe, but not to me."

"You'll see. Things will."

But it does worry me, so I say, "Maybe this stuff that's waiting to happen might go right by. Here I am already ten years old. I can't wait much longer."

I tell him how ten is the perfect age. It's a perfect number, too. I like how it looks. I'd like to be ten for a long

time. I say, "I'm going right out to look for all that stuff so
I can still be ten when something happens," but he says,
"Please wait till I get my legs back in shape."

"How did you hurt your legs? And who are you, anyway? I mean really?"

"All right, I'll tell you. You see, I was a horse once.
Actually, I *am* a horse. With four black socks. That's why
I'm called Boots."

"Yeah, yeah. Me, too." (More of a horse than he ever
was, I'll bet, and I've galloped all around here on my own
two feet.)

"I knew you wouldn't believe me, but I was, and sometimes I miss seeing all the way around behind me, though
I like looking out straight ahead, for other reasons. Eyes in
front, the world is two halves of the same thing, not two
halves of two different things like it was before. The sky,"
he says. "I used to see it from behind a tuft of grass and not
even know or care that it was the sky."

"The sky is nothing to get excited about."

"It is to me."

He gets a dreamy look and starts off on a different subject altogether. "It was hard not to just turn and run at the
slightest excuse. Even the wind. I used to run all over when
it was windy. Everything was shaking. Everything looked
scary."

(I could say all these same things about myself when I

was loping around pretending to be a horse, but I won't bother.)

"Well, I have to admit I wasn't that scared, partly it was an excuse to jump and shy. In the wind, I was always more excited than I ought to be. Running was my pleasure. Just as much fun was rolling in the dusty spots." He makes a horsey noise as if the very thought is fun. "I'd turn my tail to the storm and turn my ears away from the wind. Back then I wouldn't go near anything dead no matter what, or anywhere bears had been."

"If you were a horse, you know what? You'd be already dead, shot because of your bad legs."

"All the more reason to be a man. And how do you think I got way out here in the middle of nowhere, no clothes and all, without I was a horse?"

Then he whinnies. He starts way up high, almost a whistle, and goes way down low. He's good at it, but I can do it just as well, so I do. He laughs and I laugh, too. He puts his hand on my shoulder, as if for man to man. (Or maybe horse to horse.) I like it.

"You ought to come along with me," he says. "I could use a boy to help me out."

"Are you going somewhere? Where is it any better than right here?"

"Boy, you don't have the logic of a horse, but I do. When my legs get better, I'll show you places you wouldn't believe. You can ride me. That's a promise."

"You can't even hold yourself up."

He throws his head like a horse does when you have the reins pulled too tight. His black hair flies out behind him. I'll bet he wants me to think how like a mane it is. I have to admit there's a horsey look in his eyes, and his beard is sparse and horsey, too. He needs clipping—man or horse.

"My sister. She's always wished we had a horse. She'll like you if you're a horse, but she won't like you if you're a man."

"Then I'm just the one. So . . ." He swings his arms up on both sides, palms out. "Wish granted," he says.

I'm not sure I want my sister—my beautiful, wispy, frightened sister—riding around on somebody like Boots, who's maybe a bank robber. "I'll bet you weren't a horse. I'll bet you used to be a mule, an ugly bony old mule."

"I wouldn't mind. I have a partiality to mules."

He always says odd things. Once he picked up a stone not worth the dirt it lay on. "Rocks," he said. "They have magic. Feel how warm it is. Even now, in this cool night, it's still warm."

I don't need to know this. Anyway, I'm the one joking him more then he's joking me. I have the secret of myself, which he'll never guess in a million tries. I'm glad, because I wouldn't want to get called Girlie.

chapter two

But things happen faster than I would have thought, especially considering how nothing much has happened all this time.

Mother is sick. She's had bad spells before every now and then, so at first we don't think much of it. But then this seems worse. She's rocking back and forth and saying she's sorry to be groaning, but it makes her feel better so would we please excuse her.

It's the middle of the night. Even those mornings when my sister hitchhikes there aren't a lot of cars or buggies way out here, so I say, "I'll get the first horse I find and I can be halfway to town in an hour." But my sister says that I don't know the towns and I don't know where the doctor lives, and that I should stay with Mother. (I'm scared. I don't know what to do to help her.) My sister says for me to go get a horse and she'll ride it.

"Won't you be scared?"

"This is for Mother."

Then I get the idea of Mister Boots. I believe him—I

did all along—he really is a horse. He's still limping some, but he's much better. "I know a horse that, if you fall off, he'll stop and put you back on himself himself. I know a horse you can cluck to and kiss to or tell him in words, or point your chin to where you want to go. Moonlight Blue." (Of course Moonlight Blue. I'll have to remember to tell Boots what I named him.)

My sister says "Moonlight Blue" slowly, and gets this funny look, as if she's staring off at some sunset or other.

"I'll be back in ten minutes."

I don't know for sure if he can help us, but at least he's sort of a grown-up, and might know what to do. Well, my sister's a grown-up, all the way up to twenty, but she sure doesn't seem like it.

It's as if Moonlight Blue knew when he heard me gallop up. I got myself a neighbor's horse and rode to our tree. He's there, under the tree, looking as if straight from the moon, black mane and tail, of course four black feet. In this light, his coat is silvery, but I can see he's what they call a "flea-bit gray," which is a typical Arab color. A smallish horse, and every rib showing. I reach out, and he blows on my hand like they do. Then he whinnies. He starts way up high and goes way down. I recognize that whinny.

"Mister Boots?"

He paws the ground as horses do when they want to say, For heaven's sake, let's get on with it.

❦

My sister reaches out to let him blow on her hand. She gets an apple and splits it for him with her own teeth. She rubs his poll and down his nose. (Think of rubbing Mister Boots's poll!) After he finishes the apple, he leans low and chews at nothing to show, horse way, that he'll do anything she wants him to, and then he puts his bony forehead against her breast, which is not a good sign, so I'm glad to see my sister is just as scared to mount up as she always is.

I say, "You be careful now. I mean it!" I'm talking to Mister Boots, but my sister says, "I will."

He lopes the smoothest, most collected-up lope I ever saw, and I know my sister will be all right, at least with the riding part.

Mother is curled up on the floor by her bed. I wish she would get in it. I curl up next to her, not too close because, with all this pain, she can't bear to be touched. There's nothing I can do but worry—about her and my sister. I mean, maybe Boots *is* a bank robber. What if he runs away with her? I guess I don't really think he will, and I guess she'd have sense enough to jump off if need be. Except she might freeze up and not be able to. Except he did care about our tree.

"Roberta," my mother says.

(Roberta! This is serious.)

"There's things I have to tell you. Things I should have told you before."

Then she doesn't say anything. Later—practically a half hour later, she seems to feel a little better. She gets into bed and sips at the warm water I bring her. (That was all she wanted.) She says, "I worry about you. I don't want you to live so much in your imagination. I don't want you believing in everything you think up, like you can fly. Things are scientific."

(She tells me this all the time.) "But what were you going to tell me? You said you needed to tell me things you should have told before?"

"Oh, I'm better now, so no need. We'll pick a nice time to talk later. Just the two of us. Maybe down by the ditch."

"If you told me more things I'd know better what to believe."

"You're still so young."

"Ten," I say. "Did you forget?"

"Roberta, Roberta. I'm sorry about your name." (What does she mean by that?) "I never dared call you anything but Bobby."

She reaches toward me. (She's always a great hand-holder—when she isn't holding her knitting needles.) Now she reaches way out. "Honey . . . Roberta, you know those funny old clothes. . . ." And then she keels right over, banging her head on the floor.

I try to lift her back on the bed and when I can't, I straighten her out and put the pillow under her head. I keep calling, "Ma. Mother."

I suspect. But I don't want it to be true. Pretty soon I know for sure.

"Those funny old clothes," were her last words—but at least her next to last word was, "Roberta."

I go outside then and listen and look. First I'm listening and looking to see if my sister and the doctor and Mister Boots are coming back. I need them. But then I listen and look around at the night. We're not religious, or if we are, nobody told me, but I look at the moon and then I go down on my knees as if to some moon god. Mister Boots was right; everything is magic. I feel the breeze on my cheeks, as if it's Mother's hand.

I say, "Ma," again. I whisper it, as if I could call her back from somewhere out there. I guess I must have loved my mother. I never thought about it, but I feel sorry—sorry for myself and sorry for her because she worked so hard. Sorry I didn't help any. And maybe there was something I should have done to help her not die.

Then I think: What am I supposed to do now? Say a prayer? Wash the body? Sing a sad song? Homeschooling didn't teach me anything at all about this. But my sister should be here to sing with me, and we should wash Mother together. That's the kind of thing Mister Boots would say. So I wait. Boots said that a lot of life was being patient. I said, "Yes, if you're a horse and tied up all the time," but he said, "Every creature—people, too," and he was right.

Dawn. (Time is going by pretty fast.) The sun is just below the mountain. I want to tell Mother, "This is how it is on the morning after you died, everything pink and orange and purple. Rain over toward town, maybe on my sister and Moonlight Blue." Maybe the rain is tears. I would like a little rain. I would like to look up and have wetness on my cheeks.

"Mother, how can it be that the horned lizard by our doorstep is still alive. Even still!"

I don't seem to notice time anymore. It goes on until the sun is twelve o'clockish. I finally see the long tail of dust, and pretty soon I hear the rattle of what turns out to be the doctor's car. Mister Boots isn't with them . . . nor Moonlight Blue. Pretty soon they're close enough so I can see my sister is crying and she doesn't even know about our mother yet. Her whole front is wet even though she holds the doctor's big handkerchief wadded up against her cheeks. I get worried.

"Where is he? My Moonlight Blue?"

That starts her off even more. The doctor has to tell about it for her. "He was stolen weeks ago. Other horses escaped at that time, too. They got them all back except this one. They said his ropes and halters were still hanging there, tied to the rail. It had to be—"

My sister interrupts. "A *person*! The halters were unbuckled." Once she gets started talking, she can't stop. "They said it might have been me. After all, who needs a horse more than I do? And there I was, riding him. They say he should be shot—because of his legs. When we got to town, he collapsed. I couldn't stand for him to be shot."

"We'll take all our money—it's ours now—and buy him and pay the doctor to fix him."

But the doctor says, "Son, I saw that horse. He should be put out of his misery as soon as possible. I don't like to see an animal suffer."

"You could fix him. We'll pay."

"I don't do horses, and I'm not so sure he can be fixed. He's never going to be much good again even if his legs do heal. He's not worth two dollars. You'd have to pay two dollars to have him hauled off."

My sister says, "Moonlight Blue was sweating and shaking, but he waited till I got off before he collapsed."

"Tell me, quick, how to get there!"

"Go back with the doctor," she says. "He'll show you."

The doctor goes inside and comes right out. "She's dead," he says. He turns to me. "Did you realize that?"

My sister slumps down on her knees just like I did. Then the doctor looks more sympathetic and reaches to touch her shoulder. "I'm sorry. Can you children manage?" Then he asks my sister how old she is and when she says twenty, he says, "I thought you were hardly seventeen," and then again, "Will you manage?"

"Can I ride back with you?" I say. "I have to go for Mister . . . I mean for Moonlight Blue."

"It isn't right to go chasing after that no-good horse at a time like this."

My sister says, "That horse is special."

"Maybe he was once, but not anymore. And he doesn't even belong to you."

I ask my sister, "Where did Mother keep the money? Pay the doctor, and I'll need some more to get Moonlight back. Hurry!"

But she doesn't know where the money is any more than I do.

"But you earned half of it yourself! More than half, I'll bet! There must be some somewhere."

We look in all the normal places a person would hide money and some not-so-normal places, but we don't find a single dollar, and we don't have time to do a good job of hunting. Mister Boots might be in trouble already.

We give the doctor a white crocheted afghan for payment. It looks special, like for a wedding. I'll bet it's worth a lot more than his visit out here for no other reason than to say, "She's dead."

I gather up a few knit things in case I need to pay for Mister Boots and for a coffin for Mother. I should be thinking about her, but I hardly can because Mister Boots might be being shot right this very minute.

I ride back with the doctor. I don't like him, but I've never been in a car before. We make a nice big plume of dust.

By the time we get to town, it's evening. All the way I worry more and more about Mister Boots.

I guess if you find a man lying naked in a horse stall with ruined legs, you don't doubt at all anymore that this man is the same as that horse. Mother said I shouldn't believe things like this. Those were practically her dying words, but I just can't be the way she said to be.

At first I think he's dead, too. I know horses often die from trying too hard. But then I see the whites of his eyes flicker—catch the light for a second as he opens them a little bit.

"Mister Boots?"

Then he really looks at me and tries to speak, but only a blowy, horsey noise comes out. I get him water in the horse bucket and help him drink.

"Did I do it?"

"You did. You did." I stroke him on the shoulder like you do a horse.

"So it's all right then." And he shuts his eyes again.

His feet and ankles are so swollen I wonder if he can

stand up. I round up horse leg wraps and horse bandages and bind his feet and ankles. He grunts and throws his head back and forth. I know I'm hurting him. Then I cover him with dirty old sweat-stiffened saddle blankets to keep him warm and after that with straw to hide him.

I'm going to have to steal him some clothes all over again. Why not the doctor's? He was hardly any help at all, and yet he took that beautiful white afghan.

I tell Mister Boots I'll be right back—that I'm off to get him clothes. I'm not sure he hears me. (He's way beyond caring if he has any clothes on at all, let alone if they're nice.)

Lights are on at the doctor's house. (They have electric lights!) It's a big house, so I'm wondering, Why did he need to take that afghan when he has such a big house and car and everything?

I look in the downstairs windows. It's just the kind of thing I like to do at our house back home. I see the doctor and a wife and, off and on, a maid. I hear music. (They have a Victrola!) My mother's afghan is right there, on the wife's lap—the most beautiful thing in the room, though there's lots of beautiful things. I get sad again, thinking how my own mother made such a nice thing.

The doctor is reading the paper, but the wife is knitting! She's doing it for the fun of it. That isn't fair.

I want to hurry back to Mister Boots, but I have to do this carefully or it'll just take longer and I might get myself arrested and never get back to him. He'll starve with nothing but hay and alfalfa to eat, and if he turns into a horse again, he'll be shot first thing.

I sneak in. It's no harder than when I sneak around our own little house. (It's sometimes good being small and thin and always barefoot.) I never can sneak up on Boots, though. He has horse sense.

I take a fancy suit with a vest. I take a white shirt. He'll have clothes that match his long nose and his long slim hands.

I'm as bold as I always am. I hide in the hall closet until the doctor and his wife climb the stairs to bed. Then I hide under the back stairs and watch the maid go off to her room.

I have to wake Mister Boots again. I have to dress him all by myself, and it's hard since he's so loose and floppy. It's good the clothes are a little too wide. I forgot to get a belt so I use a halter rope. He looks dressed up except for that one thing—and his feet.

If you're stealing things anyway, you might as well steal other things to go with them. You might as well steal a big strong hairy-footed horse that can easily hold two people because I know Mister Boots can't hold himself on a horse by himself. I'm not even sure how to get him up on one. (Together we don't weigh more than one person, but I want to ride that big shire. There might never be another chance.)

"Mister Boots." I have to shout. I have to shake him. He's feverish. That's why he's so slippery. "Boots, you have to help me get you up."

He comes to a little bit. I prop him partway on the ladder to the loft. I hook his arm over the rung above him, I move the horse in close. It's the wrong side, but these big horses are the sweetest of all; they don't mind anything. What the horse will mind is that we're leaving his partner horse behind. They'll make a racket calling to each other. I hope nobody comes to check on them.

I'm not worried about being seen once we get going. I'll just say I'm helping this drunken gentleman get home after a bad night. Except I doubt if there's a single person in town who wouldn't recognize the big shire. Well, I still could be helping a drunken gentleman to get home.

Now and then Mister Boots mumbles something and I say, "What?" and he says, "I won't ride horses," and I say, "You have to, just this once."

"Take the bit out then. Use your calves."

"Calves? I thought it was my magic."

My sister is waiting for us way out by the gate. As if she's been there all this time. She's kneeling in the sand, and when she hears us clop-clopping she gets up and runs to meet us, and then walks along beside us. "Poor Moonlight Blue," she says, and then I know she knows.

"His name is *Boots*," I say. "Mister Boots."

We bring the big black shire right up to the porch steps, and lift Boots down. (Mostly we drop him.) We sort of drag him inside to the couch. After we straighten him out he does look elegant in the doctor's clothes—except for being rumpled and with straw here and there. I hadn't realized—not really—until this very minute that he could look this good.

My sister kneels beside him and kisses him and not just once. Cheeks and lips. Calls him Dear. Thank goodness he's too far gone to notice.

I suppose, with these good clothes, he's all the more attractive to her. I should have thought of that. I should have known she'd fall in love with somebody who was a horse. If I know my sister, and I do, it's too late to do anything about it—it's gimpy old Boots, too old, too thin, too odd.

I ought to be getting that big horse back (I'll be accused of stealing him *and* Moonlight Blue), but I don't want to leave my sister and Boots alone together. I want to see what's going to happen when he comes to.

"I don't think you should be kissing him like that, on the lips and all. I think you need to get to know him first."

"I do know him."

"*I'm* the one that knows him. I've helped him for weeks. I brought him food and clothes from that room."

"You gave him our father's clothes?"

"Our father! When did we ever have a father? Besides,

they're not gone, you know. Boots probably left them out under our tree. And I didn't give him fancy ones."

But then she starts to cry, for no reason. "I'm not crying," she says.

I feel like crying, too. "I know," I say. "But with Mother gone, all the more reason to be careful."

We get Boots cleaned up as best we can and covered up, then—I can't believe it—my sister measures him and starts on a sweater! (She picks red. Well, as a horse, being cream with fly-speck color, he would look good in red, but it doesn't seem right for the man.) I suppose she knits because she's nervous and knitting is her whole life. I know she was set to work knitting as soon as she could hold a knitting needle without poking her eye out. Not like me. Just knitting away and hardly even looking out the window. I never thought about it until right now.

And another thing I never thought about: our father— that I even had to have had one. Was that what Mother was about to tell me when she started out, "You know those funny old clothes. . . . "?

"Jocelyn, what about our father?"

"If Mother didn't tell you, I don't think I should say."

"For heaven's sakes, I'm ten. And that was before. Now it's just you and me."

She's sitting on the floor next to the couch, leaning her shoulder against Mister Boots's shoulder. I never saw her knitting on the floor before. I hardly ever look closely at her, but she really is beautiful. She has naturally curly hair, and now it curls all around her face, pasted to her cheeks with sweat. (I must look like our father. My hair is straight and black.) She's staring at me, thinking hard, then she says, "He never came back."

"I know that already."

I'm thinking about how those clothes are odd, like that pink turban with the jewel, and silky things, and two pairs of pants with a satin stripe along the sides.

"What was he? Why didn't Mother want me to know anything?"

"He disappeared."

"I know that! But she thought he'd come back, didn't she? Or she knew he would. Is he coming back?"

She stops knitting. "I hope," she says, and then she just sits. She looks exactly the way I feel, like everything is falling apart. "I hope," she says again, as if there never would be any, "he doesn't." She starts to knit again. She's so fast she has a couple of inches already. "He wasn't around much, but when he was, he was teaching you to be part of his magic show."

"I knew it! I knew I was magic! I always knew."

She looks at me like I'm being ridiculous, but she goes on. "Once you . . . (You were lots smaller and thinner then. We wondered if you'd live.) Once, you flew, and that one and only time, you flew away. To escape him. I didn't see it, but it had to be that. You were all the way out at the creek. Mother didn't want us to believe things like that, but how could you be that far away without flying? I found you. I brought you home. You were hardly three years old.

"When our father was here, we had plenty of money, though being poor without him is better than being rich with him. He whipped all three of us, but back when I went to school, the teacher did that all the time, too. Even the girls, though not as much. Of course our father thought you were . . . You know."

"But Mother told me over and over not to believe in things like flying."

"How else did you get way out there? You must have landed hard and broke your elbow. But sometimes I wonder if he broke your arm himself—by mistake. He wouldn't do it on purpose. He wanted you to grow up to be part of his show, but he didn't know his own strength."

Right then Mister Boots groans a long, shaky groan. My sister turns around and puts her arm across his chest. "It's all right," she says. "You're going to be fine. Just rest." She's talking to him as if to some wild animal that's hurt and frightened. My sister never has dared talk to hardly anybody, but now she goes on and on. She lifts his head and holds water to his lips. "Your feet are in bad shape, but we'll have the doctor here soon."

"What! We can't," I say. "These are the doctor's clothes."

"We have plenty of clothes." She's completely calm about it. "Help me dress him and then go take the big horse back and say we need a doctor—for a different reason."

"He won't do horses."

"Bobby!"

"And why didn't Mother ever call me Roberta?"

But Mister Boots is trying to lift himself up, not using his hands, just his elbows. His wrists are almost as badly off as his feet. My sister helps. She props him on cushions and pillows. She says, "There now. Are you in pain?"

"You're . . ." His voice is hoarse and hardly sounds out. Breathy. Wobbly. Just hearing it I would have guessed right away this was, once upon a time, a horse. "You're the one," he says. "Did I get you there?"

They look straight out at each other. My sister never does that with anybody, and horses don't usually do that unless to challenge.

"You did—of course you did." She hugs him. For heaven's sake, she would never have done that before, and she shouldn't! She's pulled his head right in close, next to her breasts. That's the second time if you count Moonlight Blue leaning against her right after she fed him apples.

"Jocelyn!" She's always shocked at me, but now it's my turn to be shocked. "You don't even know him!" But I might as well be out talking to our tree.

"Can you eat something? What do you eat?"

"He'll eat anything. I gave him Mother's stew. I gave him chicken. I'll bet he'd even eat horse meat."

Boots is still staring at my sister with his caramel-colored horse eyes, as if he can't believe she exists at all and yet here she is, existing after all.

"He's not your kind of person. He's my kind of person. Crippled forever, most likely. That's what the doctor said."

She doesn't even hear me.

She brings him an apple again and feeds him exactly as before, by hand, bite by bite. I say, "Mother's dead, for heaven's sake. She's lying in the other room, *dead*!"

"Go take the big horse back," she says, not even looking at me.

I say I will, but I don't move. I can't bear to leave them alone together. I hope Mister Boots is in bad enough shape to keep his hands off her.

Then my sister says, "Help me dress him before you go."

I don't want my sister to see him naked. How can she know what men are like, being who she is? It's different for me; I've already seen everything. And then there's all those scars he has. Should she see those?

"I'll do that by myself," I say.

"Don't be silly; we both will, and he'll help."

We undress him down to the scars—all sorts of scars. (Some have got to be horse bites.) He's not much more than a skeleton. My sister gives me a look, as if I'm to blame for something.

"I don't know about the scars, and I fed him absolutely everything I could find around. Didn't you notice the leftovers were always gone?"

"I know. It's not your fault. It's that . . . I can hardly believe it. Poor, dear horse."

Boots says, "I'm all right. I'm fine."

She picks out the fanciest of those fancy shirts, light blue with ruffles in front, and a pair of those pants with a stripe down the sides.

My sister says for me to take the doctor's clothes out to the trash bin and burn them up, but I'd hate to do that. I picked them out special. And I like how Boots looks in them, more a gentleman and not so much a circus performer. Mother would have liked them, too, because they're regular, normal clothes and yet dressy.

I take the clothes out, but I dig a shallow hole in our vegetable garden where the earth is soft. I fold the clothes up, nice and neat, and bury them.

Mister Boots is asleep when I come back in. My sister says he dropped off as soon as he ate something. She says, "So fast he nearly fell off the couch." It looks like a real sleep, so I think now would be the best time to take the big horse back to town. My sister is settled on the floor knitting again. I'll bet she'll be more than half done with that sweater by the time I get back.

"Jocelyn, there must be money here. You went to town hardly a week ago. They might charge me for using the big shire."

So we look again—all the same places we did before and different ones, too. "There has to be some. How much did you make last time?"

"Almost a hundred dollars, but I had to buy fifteen dollars' worth of yarn."

"What if we don't ever find any money? What if we're rich and don't even know it? Is that because our mother thought our father would come back and take it?"

"We'll just have to manage. I'll go on knitting, like I always do. I'll take care of you."

"I'll learn. I'll help."

"And. . . Roberta . . ." (It's as if Mother being dead made my name all right to say out loud.) "You'll have to buy a coffin."

"With what?"

"Take my order book. Perhaps the undertaker would place an order for some knitting instead of money. Tell him I'll be fast."

"You'd better make that red sweater for somebody else."

But I'm on my way out, and I don't look back. If I've made her angry, I don't want to know about it. I thought I had a secret person of my very own, and an important job helping him, and that he'd die without me, but here it is, all backward, and now he's half dead because of helping my sister.

And he'll be telling her about shying in the wind for the fun of it. I can just see them, leaning their heads together, and the horsier he is, the more my sister will love him.

When I get to town there's arguments going on all over the place, but everybody relaxes when they see me ride up on their big black horse (the shires are the most valuable things in town). When they see how I'm so willing to pay for his rental later, and how my mother died and all, and that I need a coffin, they all calm down and feel sorry for me.

I pretend I don't know anything about what could have happened to that flea-bit gray with bad legs, but they say, "Not much of a loss."

They tell me that back when my father was around, they were suspicious of my whole family, though they like my sister. Lots of people make a point of checking if she's waiting for a ride, and they pick her up whenever they see her.

"But we don't know anything about you, Boy, except we see you out by yourself in the middle of nowhere loping around as if you had someplace to go. But why did you borrow this big shire when you could have ridden home on something smaller?"

I say, "I never got to be with a horse as big as this before." And that's the honest truth.

The doctor thinks I'm the one who stole his clothes, but since I went straight to his house and asked him to come back to ours, he's not sure. But he doesn't want to come anyway. "That's a godforsaken place," he says. "It's a long way, and I've already been out there once for nothing."

"Don't you think that white afghan is worth enough for a little bit more?"

"Well . . . but it better be for a good reason."

"It will be. I promise."

I get to have another ride in the doctor's car, and this time I pay more attention and enjoy it. I ask a lot of questions about how much it cost and how much gas costs, and that makes the doctor happy.

"Now this one . . . It's not like just any car around. It cost a bundle. You can snap the windows in and out. . . ."

There's some cows on the road when we're partway home, and I yell, "A-*ooo-ga*," out the window, and they move right off. I sound exactly like a real horn. I do it when we get close to our house, too, so the doctor doesn't have to honk his horn to let my sister know we're here. The doctor doesn't even thank me for honking for him. I guess he thinks I'm making a lot of racket for somebody whose mother just died.

Every so often I catch myself making a mistake about myself, and it's not all my fault. Here I am thinking: When I grow up to be a man, I'll get myself a car like this one. But right after, I wonder if women ever have them. If they don't, I could be the first.

I can smell the strong smell of valerian tea even before the doctor and I go in the door. Mister Boots is awake, lying propped up on cushions and pillows, and my sister sits beside him rubbing his head just above his ears as if he's still a horse. It's so clear I think the doctor will see right away how this is the ruined horse that collapsed practically at his door . . . the scraggly horse beard, the scraggly mane. . . . (His hair is exactly the length of a mane.) And the doctor does look shocked, but then he says, "Is this your father?" so I know he's shocked by the clothes. Which is my sister's fault.

My sister says, "Of course not." Louder than necessary.

"Well then, who is this man? There's no circus around here. Where'd he come from?"

I give my sister a look. What's she going to answer to that?

"He's a friend of our father's. . . ." She says it as if it's a question.

"I hope this man isn't like him."

"Oh, he isn't! He *can't* be!"

The doctor does what he has to do—and gently. He gives us a bottle of painkiller for nothing, so I guess he's not so bad. Maybe he likes me better because I asked so many questions about his car and how to drive and how hard it is to find gas stations.

He's going to take Mother to the undertaker. He tells us not to watch, but I do. I want to be sure he treats her properly. He wraps her up in a sheet and puts her in his car. Jocelyn gives him Mother's best dress for the undertaker to dress her in.

Then he comes back to talk to me privately. I suppose since I'm the boy. He leans close and whispers, "That man will be a cripple for the rest of his life. You'd best be prepared. I'll come again sometime next week and see how he's getting along, and check up on both of you, too."

(To think my sister has already ridden Boots, but I never have and now I probably never will, even though he promised.)

chapter three

That night we build a fire in the fireplace. We all get a little drunk, my sister and me on sherry we found when we didn't find the money, and Mister Boots on his pain medicine. My sister sits on the floor, knitting again. Every now and then she reaches up to give Boots a pat on the shoulder. I'm lying flat out on the rug Mother crocheted, and all of a sudden here's Mister Boots, telling us his story. To Jocelyn. In all this time, he hardly even began to tell it to me. At first, as usual, I can't make out what he's talking about.

He says, "Please excuse me," and my sister says, "What for?" and he says, "For how I am," and my sister says, "Of course," and he says, "I mean *really*," and, "It's that I know other things. Stallions." He thinks about it and then says, "Pitted against each other. I have the scars. And I wasn't lazy. I never understood why they beat me. They raced us, too."

He sits up and puts his bandaged feet on the floor. My sister stops knitting. She touches his knee. "It's all right now," she says. "You won't have any of that again."

"Of course we all did love to race. Even out in the pasture we'd race for no reason. Some horses stood up for each other, but not a single human being stood up for me. But then there was one, and—" he looks over at me "—and then there was you."

He stops and puts his head back on the pillow and his feet back up and starts again, so quietly I have to move closer and my sister leans her head on the same pillow, right up next to his. He's talking in a whispery way that makes it magic. I wouldn't dare interrupt.

He grunts a couple of horsey grunts, and I'm wondering if he's still in pain even though he's drunk from that painkiller. "Those men had whips as long as three horses. They snapped. Lots of times not over my head. One night, after the worst . . . something happened. It was from panic.

"I turned boy, escaped between the bars of the round pen, ran, and hid inside a gunnysack. But I turned colt again as soon as my terror died. They brought me back and terrified me worse than ever. But there would be another time." He's out of breath just telling about it. "Give me a sip of your sherry."

He blows out a great, loose-lipped horse breath right into her glass! Doesn't he know *anything*? Well, I guess he doesn't. How could he? Who would have told him?

"And then tied up," he says, "all day long. Sometimes in the sun. Nothing to do but learn to untie myself. Even as a horse I could do that. Lots of us could. We had plenty of time to learn it."

"I would hate that," I say.

"I did, too, but the panic was worse. A time did come when I changed out of terror again. I knew what to do this time. I ran, first as boy, and then for a long time as horse, long and hard and up into the mountains. When the going got too rough and steep and frightened me as a horse, then as a boy—until I ran into a man, his arms around me as I fell. I was too tired to care that this was, yet again, a man.

"That man couldn't bear to be with people, but he was happy to be with me, boy *or* colt. Neither of us understood what I was, but he knew me right away. Or cared about me, which is the same thing and just as good. He held me on his lap until I stopped trembling. Stroked me, groomed me, both as boy and colt. His was the first love I ever got from a human being. All I know I learned from him. Except how to hear and smell and listen. I knew all those better than he did.

"You'd think, with all that galloping around in pastures . . ." He shakes his head, up and down like a horse would. "You'd think when I think of freedom it would be as a horse . . . built for speed, born for speed and nothing other. You'd think it would be as a horse that I would feel free, but never so, sad to say.

"At first I thought the part being a boy was the dream, and after that I thought the horse part was the dream—of speed and flying, as if a horse could be a bird. I thought I had been a person from the start, and only thought myself a horse, just as you do, Boy. But why would I daydream so much terror?" He rolls his big horse eyes. "I rubbed the skin off my chest and shoulders. I cut my lips. One time I jumped, but landed *on* the fence, only halfway out."

My sister leans her head into the couch cushions and begins to cry. Mister Boots turns and nibbles at her neck. I'm wondering if he knows how to kiss? It looks like he doesn't.

Then my sister turns and they're cheek to cheek, nuzzling and nibbling like horses do, even my sister. I'm not sure, but I think he licked her neck. I don't know what to do to stop it.

"Mister Boots, I'm not a boy, you know. Mister Boots. Mister Boots. I'm not a boy."

Nobody is listening.

My sister says, "I don't want you ever hurt," and I say, "Moonlight Blue is a horse and did you see his color? Flea-bit, flea-bit. That's really what they call it. Sometimes they even call it fly-specked."

"Moonlight Blue," she says, as if it's the most beautiful name there ever was. (Does she know it was me thought that name up? But then I never told her.) "Moonlight Blue. I love you, Moonlight Blue."

Mister Boots says, "I felt a bird inside my chest the first time I saw you." And Jocelyn says, "Oh yes. Oh yes."

So they lean against each other until Mister Boots falls asleep again or maybe passes out from the painkiller. My sister keeps patting him like she forgot she was doing it, but she finally turns back to her knitting.

I'm resigned—to everything. What else is there to do? I tell my sister I want to help knit things so we can get some more money, but she says she doesn't have the time to teach me now. Maybe later. She says she could knit three things in the time it would take her to teach me to do one messy, no-good thing. Except all she's doing is just knitting this red sweater for Mister Boots. If she goes on like this, she'll never make any money.

"I've heard tell horses can't even see red anyway."

"I like it," she says. "It fits with how he looks."

I guess I'll go off and look for money-hiding places. That's more practical than what she's doing.

I wish she wasn't so beautiful. She could have any boy she wanted if only she didn't always hide in her hair. If she was ugly I wouldn't mind her loving Mister Boots. I'd think he was all the love she could ever get.

But I don't go look for the money. I go outside in the dark and pick up another little nothing pebble. I hug it in both hands. I want to make it feel comfortable. I think how holding my pebble is just as if I held a star. I know that's not even a little bit true (it isn't that my mother and my sister haven't homeschooled me enough—too much in fact), but I like thinking it. I lie down on the sand and put the pebble in my mouth. We never have candy. I can't remember last time I had some. (After I find the money, I'm going to sneak some for candy.) Then I almost swallow the pebble, so I take it out and put it in my belly button to keep it warm. It fits perfectly. I squint to make the stars funny and fuzzy. I hold my breath and tense up all my muscles and think hard. If I once was so magic I could fly, I ought to be magic enough to find our money.

Just then an owl flies right over me. Utterly silent. Utterly magic. I see the white underbelly. I feel him, too— the rush of air. I think about flying, how I could raise my arms and lift myself right up. I think I'm floating away, but I fall asleep by mistake. I know I just dream it.

My sister must have knit all night. When I wake up and go inside, Mister Boots is wearing the red sweater and my sister is shaving him . . . shaving off those sparse, coarse, horsey whiskers. She says she's not going to cut his hair. She's keeping it like a mane. After she shaves him, my sister begins knitting him a pair of socks. I wonder if she's ever going to get back to knitting for us to sell?

(Could my sister have a horse baby? Could that really happen? Good thing a foal's hooves are soft at first.)

⚬⚮⚬

Mister Boots is as curious as a horse. As soon as he can hobble around holding on to walls, he examines our house. He says he's only been in two houses in his whole life. That's not so odd, I've hardly been in more than that myself. He leans close. Blows. Licks. Nibbles. Tastes. It's a good thing Mother isn't here to watch. She'd say he's getting germs all over. And she wouldn't like the way he pries into drawers and boxes, and how he lies down on all the beds, even my little one (which nobody fits but me). When he was out with that man who helped him, he slept on hay. They both did. Back then Boots never even knew there were such things as beds.

I found out that he can't read. I brought him my book, *Black Beauty*. I thought maybe, since Mister Boots was mostly just lying around recovering, he'd read to me some evenings, but I'm the one who has to read to him. We hardly have any books. We're too poor. There's Jocelyn's old learning-to-read books that I learned on, there's a dictionary, and there's one really good book called *Smoky the Cow Horse*. I've read that a dozen times.

I haven't been out to water my tree lately, so I decide I should go. I'll bet water to a tree is like candy to a person. I'll bet the tree sucks it in real slow to make it last a long time.

I usually go at night when I can secretly borrow

somebody's horse, but this time I borrow one in daylight—Rusty, the pony. From what they said in town it's never been a secret, anyway.

When I get close I see a horse and a tent, and when I get closer I see that it's a *very* nice horse. Then a man comes out of the tent, and it's just the opposite of when I found Mister Boots. This man's all dressed up in fancy clothes, riding britches, and shiny English-type boots. The man's too soft and too fat, but the horse is in good shape—probably from having to carry a fat man around all the time.

The man has shiny, Japanese-ish hair, a showy little mustache, and a teeny, useless little goatee. Everything shiny black. He says a fancy "*Good* morning," and gives me a fancy, phony smile.

I don't answer. I get off the horse and, real quick, pour the water down at the tree roots. He's not going take any water away from my tree. Besides, a man like this will have canteens.

So then he says, "What's your name, Sonny?"

I already know who this is, and even *he* thinks I'm a boy. Was I even Mother's secret? I don't know if I should answer, so I don't.

"So your mother's dead?"

It's *sort* of a question, but I know he knows, and that's why he's here. All of a sudden I wonder if he knows where the money is. Maybe he came for it.

"How old are you now? Seven? Eight?"

I know I'm small for my age, but can't he keep track of *anything*? I'm not going to answer, and that's that.

He starts gathering his things and tying them on his horse. I jump back on Rusty. She's small enough that I don't need to put her in a low place for getting on. (I shouldn't think "jumped on her." I really pulled myself up by her mane, which, since she's a pony, she doesn't have much of.)

"That your pony? Your mother must be making money to have a nice horse like that."

I do answer. "She doesn't belong to us. We don't have a horse. We're too poor."

I'm wondering, Can we get hold of this fancy one he's riding? Mister Boots won't be any good to us as a horse—if as anything at all but another mouth to feed.

I wait while our father packs up his tent and mounts up, and we head for the cottage. He rides in front, and he sure knows the way. When we're almost there, I jump off Rusty and put her in the neighbor's pasture where she belongs. Then I walk along behind our father. My sister comes out to the porch. She heard the horse, and she knows somebody riding up on a horse isn't going to be me; I never ride all the way in. When she sees our father she just stands and stares. She looks *wonderful*! All of a sudden taller— standing straight for a change—and her mussed-up hair all golden in the sun. She has her knitting needles in her hand.

The way she's holding them makes her look dangerous. I realize she's not as helpless as she's always seemed to be. Yes, I think, yes! *My* sister!

Our father dismounts and walks toward her holding his arms out as if to hug her, but she steps back. The way she looks now, nobody would dare hug her.

"Everything I did was for your own good. That's the only reason I ever did anything. And look at you now."

My sister turns away.

"So where's your mother?"

She knows he knows, just like I did. So then our father walks right in, thumping down hard on the porch boards with the heels of his fancy English riding boots.

Of course who's in there is Mister Boots, dressed in our father's clothes. He's lying with his bandaged feet propped up on cushions and the couch arm, but when our father comes in, he sits up fast, and carefully doesn't look him in the eyes. That's the horse way, so as not to challenge.

Our father stares though. He's taking in his own old circus-type clothes—how they droop on Boots and are too short. How his fancy alligator belt has a hole punched in it to make it smaller.

He doesn't say anything. He just grunts and goes back to Mother's bedroom and then comes right out again, asks, straight at Mister Boots, "Where is she!" as if Boots had hidden her away. Our father looks like he's going to punch

Mister Boots, so my sister says, "She's at the undertaker in Tungsten Town."

"Well . . ." Our father plops down in our only over-stuffed chair. He looks relieved. "So she really is dead then."

Had I thought at all about having a father, he's not the sort I would ever have wanted. His eyes are squinty, and his cheeks are chubby (having a goatee doesn't help at all). His thighs must be as big around as my waist.

"I guess you're not so glad to see me. I can understand that, but things will be better with me here."

"But you . . . You . . . All of us . . ." My sister's so upset she can't talk. She has tears in her eyes again, but this time from frustration—maybe at herself for not being able to say anything at all.

"I never did one single thing that wasn't for your own good. Take this boy, here. From the very start he disobeyed everything we said. Remember? Tore up books, unraveled knitting, even played with fire. It's a wonder he hasn't burned the house down by now. There wasn't anything bad he didn't do. Look," he says, and bares his forearm. "He bit me. Look at these teeth marks. And here on my hand, too. You were a big girl then, what? Ten . . . twelve years old? You remember all that."

(Maybe she does, but I don't remember any of it. And I wouldn't have torn up books. Would I? Is that why we hardly have any?)

My sister *is* impressive. I used to think "wishy-washy
and dishwater blond," but now I think "golden lion-type
hair." She looks like she might even yell out "Bullshit!" like
those wranglers at the next-door ranch do. I wish she
would.

What she does is snort. She sounds as much like a horse
as Boots does.

"Who is this man here?" Our father is pointing at
Mister Boots as if to shoot him with a finger. "What has
this man got to do with your mother? Where is this man
sleeping? Are you married? I never heard about it."

"When would you hear anything?"

Are we about to have a fight? I'll help.

But I guess I must be nervous because I hop and jump
and cavort around. Then I laugh like a crazy person, and I
give this screech. It makes everybody jump. I remember I
used to do that a lot a long time ago, to scare people. I forgot all about it. I don't know what I'm trying to do now.
Maybe I want to be as bad as our father says I used to be.

He sits up straight and frowns at me. "There now,
what did I tell you? *Discipline!* Like I always say." He slaps
his hand hard on his own knee, as if it's instead of hitting
me. Then he turns to my sister and whispers, "I never lose
my temper. Never!" He settles back, his fat knees wide
apart. "Never!" Then he asks if there's any beer around,
but we haven't ever had any such thing as beer or liquor,

just that little bit of sherry we found and drank all up. I don't need to wonder anymore what it's like to get drunk.

"There used to be some brandy," our father says. "Trust your mother to have poured it on the grapevines."

"No, *I* did that," I say, and giggle.

My sister doesn't know what to make of me. I cross my eyes at her, but *I* don't know what to make of me either. She sits down next to Mister Boots. She pats his shoulder as if to calm him. The way his hair hangs over his forehead, half to one side and half to the other . . . I've seen the exact same thing with horses. It always gives them a mild, sweet look. Even so, right now, he doesn't look so mild. "Easy, easy," my sister says, exactly as you say to a horse. She turns to our father. "You came back because Mother's dead. We're fine."

(Does she mean even with no mother and no money?)

Our father takes out a partly smoked cigar, lights it, and puffs out a smelly cloud. Mister Boots moves to the far end of the couch and blows a blustery horse blow.

"You need me. I would never leave you children out here by yourselves."

"Need you!" My sister turns around and pulls up her blouse to show her bare back. She has some of those exact same scars. No wonder she doesn't like men. So then what about Mother? If Mother has them, the undertaker will know all about it. But it won't be the first time he's seen that. I've seen scars on those wranglers next door when I watch them wash up in the cow pond. Not just on the black men, but the white men, too, though not quite as bad. (They don't care about me watching. They all think I'm a boy.)

Mister Boots looks at my sister's back and then he turns and stares at our father. I know that stare, that lowered head, but our father doesn't get the message. I've never seen Boots look like this. His face is as impassive as a horse's always is to humans, but I can almost see Moonlight Blue with his ears plastered back. Can't our father see that?

Our father doesn't seem to care that my sister's back looks terrible. He shakes his head as if to say, Yes, yes, I know all that. And I guess he does. "Well," he says, "if no brandy, how about some coffee then?"

My sister says she's already served him often enough when she was six years old and even younger, and she isn't going to do it anymore.

But I think, How about pouring boiling hot coffee on our father's head, and then how about we all jump him and hold him and maybe whip him so he'll have the same marks all over him that we have on us? Except he probably has them already.

"I'll get it," I say, but my sister shouts, *"Don't!"*

Mister Boots hasn't moved from his ready-to-attack position. Or is it ready-to-run? That's what horses always do first.

But nobody is *doing* anything. I'm beginning to suspect it might be all up to me. Besides, I'm the only one with any luck.

"I'm going to get the coffee," I say. I need for something to be happening. I start to jump—jump and jump and jump toward the kitchen. It's not easy. Why in the world am I doing this? The good thing about it is, everybody is looking at me and wondering about me. I want to go on acting crazy. Or maybe I want to go slowly so my sister can stop me just in case I'm doing the wrong thing, and she does get up to do that.

Our father says, "Good boy." He gets up, faster than you'd think a fat man would, and grabs my sister's arm and twists it up behind her so she gasps and has to lean way down as if she has a stomachache.

Then I remember. I've had this dream, over and over, my arm twisted exactly like that. I'll bet I didn't fly like my sister said I did. I'll bet our father broke my elbow just this way. If I was only three years old, it probably wouldn't have taken much twisting to do it.

I keep on jumping and jumping, and when I'm in the kitchen, I stop. I stir the fire in the stove and throw on kindling, and then I stand still and listen. I hear my sister gasp again. I feel bad for her, and I feel bad that I'm not strong enough to rescue her.

And then—but I didn't see any of it. I hear a clatter

that sounds like hooves on our wood floor. I hear our father make a funny noise. I go back in and everybody is sitting exactly as before, except not a single person looks the same. My sister is next to Mister Boots on the couch holding Boots's wrist. Boots is staring at his bandaged feet. Our father is in the chair, again lounging back, except it doesn't look like lounging anymore. It looks . . . Well, he's kind of shriveled.

Boots couldn't have, could he? I mean he couldn't change just for half a minute—just time enough to stamp around—and then change back again so fast?

Our father looks at me and says, "I thought you went for coffee." His voice sounds as if he's suddenly caught a cold. He's staring down at that little round rug Mother hooked that has birds all over it and is so pretty. We always keep it in front of that big chair. There's not much around here Mother didn't make.

I say, "Oh," and go back to get the coffee. This time I walk like a normal person. I still don't know if I'll pour the whole pot of boiling coffee on our father's head or not.

I'm beginning to remember all those things I used to do when I was little and everybody said I was a handful. I *did* mess things up, but it must have been only when our father was here.

Anyway, my very own father doesn't know how old I am and that I'm not a boy! Maybe my mother and my sister tried to fool him. Maybe he wouldn't have wanted me if I wasn't a boy. All the babies in the graveyard are boys and he already had my sister so maybe he didn't want any more like her.

I bring the coffee, all very normal, on a tray and with oat cookies my sister made for Mister Boots. (Boots doesn't like coffee, so I brought him tea. I brought myself cider but in a cup so it looks like coffee, so my sister will be mad at me.

Nobody says anything; we all just eat and sip. And pretty soon my sister gets up to get supper, which is nothing but beans. We don't have any money for really good food. This is the best we have. I used to think everybody in the world ate mostly beans, but by now I know beans are a dead giveaway to how poor a person is. It'll especially be a dead giveaway when we have beans again tomorrow.

(I never saw a person eat so much so fast as our father. We could have had three more meals on his just one.)

We have this little table in our little kitchen. Hardly room enough for four. We don't have a dining room. We have a sitting room and then the little kitchen with worn-out linoleum, which I never noticed how worn-out till right now. But we have a nice big window over the sink with very nice curtains Mother made. They have ducks on them.

We've been eating without any talking when all of sudden my sister asks our father if he knows where any money might be. I wish she hadn't said anything. If she wanted to ask things, she should have come to me and discussed it first, because if our father knows where any money might be, he'll just take it for himself. I'll bet that's why he came back.

And then he practically says it—at least that he did it before. "Why, I took the money with me." Then he smiles around at each of us. "I was off all the way to New York. To make money for the family. I knew you'd get along. Even then your mother was knitting away so fast you wouldn't believe it."

New York! That's a long way from us here in California.

Our father eats his last few bites standing up, washes everything down with coffee, and then goes (of course) into that never-used room.

(We hadn't even thought of putting Mister Boots in there. I guess both my sister and I wanted him handy in the living room, not shut away down the hall in that back bedroom. Besides, it's a terrible mess; you can't even get to the bed, partly because we've been looking for the money in there and then because my sister has been rummaging around in the clothes to find things for Mister Boots. Not a single one of us ever cleaned up in there. We just kept the door shut.)

Our father looks shocked the minute he steps in. I start to giggle even before he opens the door, and I can't stop. I have to go outside or else I'll burst.

I sit on our front step, my hand over my mouth. Mister Boots ought to be out here—all his talk of breezes on cheeks and skies that go on forever. I'd help him to come out, but I have to get rid of my giggles first. I keep giggling until suddenly I start to cry—for no reason whatsoever. For a while, it's either cry or giggle. Finally it stops.

When I go back and check that room again, it looks as if our father has had a fit in there. Even what was hanging in the closet is on the floor. I hear a lot of thumping and scraping, and I see right away where the secret hiding place is. There's a trapdoor in the ceiling of the closet. Our father is up there cursing. I've heard the wranglers next door say lots of things. I was hoping to learn more words, but our father doesn't say anything I haven't heard already.

Of course my first thought is to close the hatch and lock him up up there, but the hatch is on the closet floor and I can't figure out how to do it.

My second thought is that Mother would never have gone up there, so *our* money can't be up there. I mean, Mother never even went in that room that I know of. If she had, she'd have cleaned it up a long time ago.

Our father throws down an oblong box. Dust flies up when it hits the floor, and it gets even more broken than it already is. You can see where it used to be red with gold designs, but the colors are almost all worn off. The lid is just barely hanging on, and there's something odd about the bottom, as if there's two bottoms. Then he jumps down, carrying a smaller, square box as worn out as the bigger one, and it looks to have two bottoms, too, and one's a mirror. The money has got to be someplace like that, a secret extra bottom.

"So where is it?" our father says. He's dusty and sweaty and streaked with dirt.

"Well, it's not up there."

"I know that." He looks at me like he knows I'm guilty—like it's *always* got to be me. So then *I* start thinking it's got to be me, too. I'm the one who does all the bad things around here. Except I don't know where anything is, money or brandy or anything. The trouble is I say I know. "Buried in the yard," I say, "in the nice soft dirt of the vegetable garden. Seventh carrot."

Our father gets his face up real close to mine. He smells of fat-man sweat and cigars. I turn away because of that, so then his hot sloppy whisper gets right inside my ear. "And you're the one who's going to dig it up."

I twist away and run. I get to the field next door, grab a fence post, vault the barbed wire, jump on Rusty, and gallop off.

Our father's horse is right there by the door, all cinched up and ready. I'm just riding a pony. He's going to catch me, and we're going to be out here all alone. But I keep on, and when I get to my tree, I don't get off, I just reach up

and grab the first branch as we gallop by and start climb-
ing. I'm thinking how good I am at things like this and
how no fat man can get me. But our father does exactly the
same thing. I thought he was too big and soft for that. Then
I think if I get high enough, the branches will be small and
our father will fall.

"Where there's a will there's a way," our father says.

Oh, for heaven's sake, I've heard Mother say the same
thing, too often, though mostly she said, "Well begun is
half done," and of course most of all, "A stitch in time . . ."
I've heard Mister Boots say the same sorts of things, except
Boots's were odder, as if a horse had made them up all by
himself. Like, "When we want enough, we get a little." I'm
sick of *all* those things.

I thought my tree would save me by breaking itself. It's
not easy getting water way out here. I thought it would do
something for me for a change. I know this is exactly the
kind of thinking Mother didn't want me to do when she
told me to be scientific, but I thought it anyway.

Some branches do break, but not enough. Our father
grabs me by the ankle in no time and pulls me down to
him. Even before we're on the ground, he twists my arm up
behind me.

"I'll let go when you say you'll come down quietly like
a good boy for once in your life and go dig up the money."

I say, "Why not?"

"Promise."

I don't want to promise anything I won't keep. I just say, "Of course." That's not really a promise. I didn't say, of course *what*.

Rusty has run off to a nice grassy spot, but our father's horse is still there, obediently ground-tied.

I ride behind our father. It's good I'm small. The poor horse has enough to do with our father on him.

We pace. Nice and smooth and fast. I thought so. I knew this horse was a harness racer from the bit our father used. You're not supposed to ride those.

I ask what the horse's name is, but our father just grunts a whole batch of angry grunts. I wonder what he'll think when I dig up the doctor's fancy clothes instead of money.

When we get back, our father keeps a good hold on me and starts me digging.

I see my sister staring out the kitchen window at us. She was washing the dishes and saw us right away. Our father sees her, too, so I feel a little bit safer.

The doctor's clothes aren't hard to dig up. I just heeled them in until I'd have time to take them to a better spot. I think to run the minute a little bit of them shows, but our father has his eye on me. I just go on digging until the clothes are completely out. I pick them up and shake the dirt off so he can see they're not bags of money.

He gets this funny look. Then he slaps my cheek. Says,

"What's going on? Why are these buried? Where's the body?" Things like that. But the way he's bouncing me around, I couldn't answer if I wanted to.

Then my sister is there, and Mister Boots is hobbling out behind her.

And there our father goes with my arm up behind me again. "Keep back," he says, "or else."

My sister and Mister Boots grab each other to hold each other back. My sister says, "Easy. Nice and easy," as if trying to slow down a horse that's going a little bit too fast, but Mister Boots is standing as still as could be, though he's trembling. My sister is, too. I can see the bottom of her skirt shake.

"Pick up those clothes," our father tells me, "and we're all going inside. Quietly and calmly. You two first."

They go and stand in the doorway, but *we* go to his horse, where some stuff is still tied on his saddle. (I'm thinking about what Boots said about being tied up for hours, and how this horse still has a tight cinch, too.) Our father keeps hanging on to me, so he has to do everything one-handed. He reaches in his saddlebag and takes out a pistol.

Would he shoot his very own child? And especially would he shoot me if he thinks I'm a boy?

He sticks the pistol in his belt and then takes out a black stick thing with silvery edges. It looks like a quirt, only it isn't. He points it at me as if it's the pistol. I know

what it is. I remember from a long time ago. A magic
wand. He points it at me and grins a big grin like, Now I've
got you. "Blam," he says. "Blam, blam, blam." Then he
laughs and it's like I not only inherited his black Japanese
hair, but that high-pitched, stupid laugh. I will never laugh
again, not like that anyway, even if I have to go out in the
desert to practice up a new one.

"Mother didn't believe in magic wands," I say.

"She didn't believe in me either, but I'm here, big as
life." (Bigger, I'm thinking, bigger and fatter than life.)
"And I kept you all in lots more than beans." He waves the
wand right close to my face, and flowers pop out of it. So
fast they hit me in the eye, and so many and such big ones
you'd think . . . you'd *know* they couldn't come out of that
narrow tube. Except they don't smell good. They make me
sneeze. But what about Mother! All the things she said not
to believe in are true.

I reach to take the flowers. Since they came out of thin
air, why would he need them back when it's so easy to get
more? But he snatches them away and stuffs them in the
saddlebag, so then I know they can't be real or they'd be
ruined in there. No wonder they smell bad; they're old.

Our father puts the magic wand in his belt beside the
pistol. He's pretty good when you think he's doing all this
with just one hand, and that I've wiggled all around and
sneezed a whole half dozen times.

My sister and Mister Boots are still in the doorway watching. I have to admit they look good together.

"Hold your horses," our father says. (Does he know!) "Now everybody just go in and sit down."

We sit exactly as before. Our father lets go of my arm and holds me between his knees instead. "Watch," he says. Then . . . One minute his hands are empty and the next a flame flies out—flies across the room and hits the far corner wall. We all jump, but Mister Boots shies practically out the door. You'd think he'd be ashamed, except he didn't shy as much as most horses would from a flash of fire. Most would be gone.

"Now," our father says again. He lets me go and sits, legs as wide apart as before, the knees of his riding britches nice and snug, but his crotch drooping, the pistol and the magic wand tucked right out in front. He smiles around at everybody. "Now listen, I'm going to take this boy here along with me. All the way to Los Angeles. I need him. He'll get to see the world. Get to ride *real* horses. Maybe drive my trotter. I'll teach him all the tricks. He'll wear decent clothes and eat decent food. Lots of oranges and no more beans.

"Boy," he says, and turns to me, "I'll raise you up in the air, with, like they say, no visible means of support. Only you will know how it's done. You'll have a nice costume. Any color you want." Then he says, "Lassiter and Son," three times.

All of a sudden I want to go. I don't care that I don't

like him, or even that he'll twist my arm behind me. I want to make flowers pop out of things. I want to throw fire. I want to go so badly I start feeling sick to my stomach.

My sister shouts a great big, *"No!"*

"I'll go instead," Mister Boots says. "I'm used to this kind of thing."

My sister shouts about a dozen no's in a row.

"This boy's wasting his life out here." (Yes, I am. I always knew it.) "And he wants to come." He turns to me. "You'll like it. You'll be around men. Now you go shake these clothes out real good for me, boy. I want to try them on. They're high-quality clothes."

He takes the pistol from his belt, aims out the door, and shoots. Right through the screen. Outside a puff of sand flies up, and Mister Boots shies again. It's good he's not being a horse and nobody is riding him. They'd have fallen off for sure.

"Nervous fellow," our father says. (Of course he's nervous, what horse isn't?) Then, "You just all sit quietly while I go get dressed."

When he's gone, we look at one another. My sister shakes her head. "Like he says, we'll all sit quietly. We don't want anybody shot."

I say, "I want to throw fire."

My sister says, "Think, for heaven's sake! Remember who you are!"

"I *am* thinking."

When our father comes back, he does look impressive. "Now then . . . Mister Boots, is it? Now Mister Boots, I want to know how you did that trick earlier today? Projections? Mirrors? I didn't quite catch it."

What if Boots doesn't know what he's not supposed to say? I have to change the subject.

"I *do* want to go with you," I say. "I want to learn how to throw fire."

"Good boy."

"Bobby!"

I notice my sister isn't calling me Roberta. More and more I'm thinking all this must have started way back with Mother. I'm glad. I like having secrets, but I like *being* a secret even more.

"Think a minute. *Think*," she says, standing up and looking at me. "You can't. You know perfectly well you can't."

So then I *do* think, and what I think is: Yes I can. I haven't had any trouble being a boy so far, and I haven't even tried. I know our father wouldn't want me if he knew I was a girl. My sister knows that, too. She could have stopped all this right then with that one single word: Roberta.

"There are no magicians like there used to be." Our father is sounding kind of dreamy. "No one anymore at all like me. I'll teach you, boy. Hundreds of secrets.

Thousands." He's nodding to himself, and he has this little satisfied smile. He looks as if everything is exactly the way he wants it, but then he says, "The money," and keeps on nodding and smiling to himself. "The money."

I don't know why he needs our money, what with his fancy horse and fancy boots and clothes. He has to be rich enough already.

"I told you," my sister says, "we can't find it. We've looked all over. All of us."

"We'll see," our father says. "I'm not in any hurry."

I can't wait until I can get off alone and check for false bottoms or odd mirrors. I can't tell my sister. She shouldn't know these magic things. Our father told me not to tell anybody about those boxes. He said magicians have to swear not to tell and he said, now that I know, I have to swear it, too, and not even tell my sister. He said, "What's the use of magic if everybody knows about it?" It's easy to see that that's the exact truth.

chapter four

Right then, we hear the doctor's *a-ooo-ga, a-ooo-ga* coming down our little road. We'd have known he was coming anyway because he rattles. We all stand up, and my sister looks at me hard. I look cross-eyed at her again, and I start to giggle. Now we'll see about those clothes.

Our father hides his pistol and his magic wand under the chair cushion.

I got to like the doctor a little bit, little by little. Maybe he got to like us little by little, too. He did a lot of good things. I hope he doesn't get hurt. I'll jump in front if our father takes out the pistol.

The doctor's not even all the way in the door when he stops, shocked, and says, "So it was you! All this time, you!" And then, "You're their father. I've heard about you."

Why would he guess right away that this greasy-haired fat man is our father? Unless I look like him some way I don't know.

I'm mixed up because, on the one hand, I'm glad our

father is getting blamed for stealing the clothes, but, on the other hand, I don't want him hauled off to jail just when I was about to go with him and learn to be even more magic than I already am.

The doctor walks right in, and there they are, belly to belly—both of them as well dressed as anybody I ever saw. Our father and the doctor are about the same size, and they look kind of alike except the doctor has white hair and is mostly bald.

"This is disgraceful," the doctor says.

"What are you talking about?" our father asks.

"Unconscionable." The doctor swings around as if he can't stand the sight of our father. He's so angry he can't contain himself. I think maybe he'll hit our father, but instead he does the opposite; he gets himself all calmed down (you can see him doing it, taking a big breath), then he goes to Mister Boots. "Let me see your ankles."

He helps Boots lie down with his feet on the cushions, and he pulls up the footstool, sits there, and examines him. First I thought he'd be so mad he might be rough by mistake, but he's about as gentle as I ever saw anybody be. He bandages Boots in clean bandages. And tells him, "For heaven's sake, stay off your feet!" Then he turns to my sister. "He must, you know. It's important. And, my dear, there's something else." (You can tell he likes my sister.) "They have your mother in a nice box. Do we bury her out here with the dead babies, or—" he turns to our father, suddenly angry again "—cremate her and put her in a jug on the mantel? What do you expect me to do, just stand here and let all this go by as if nothing has happened? And another thing, the undertaker says your wife had marks of being whipped. That isn't done anymore nowadays. I'd like to take a look at these children."

If I'm going to go on being a boy, he mustn't do that.

Our father's looking more and more nervous. "You have to agree children are little savages."

"What about the clothes? The clothes?"

Our father looks as innocent as he really is.

"What have you got to say for yourself?"

"I don't know what you're talking about."

"My clothes. What are you doing wearing my clothes?"

Our father gets this funny look, like, Oh! He looks down at himself as if he's surprised at what he has on. Then he looks back at the doctor, and there's no doubt that these clothes belong to the doctor. They're exactly like what he already has on—same exact gray—except the vest is tan on the doctor and cream-colored on our father. I picked the cream-colored one specially for Boots. I knew he'd look good in it.

Nobody is paying any attention to me. I sidle over to where the pistol's hidden under the cushion. My clothes— those old cut-off men's overalls I wear—leave a lot of room to put things. They have man-sized pockets back and front.

"What in the world were your clothes doing buried out in our vegetable garden?"

They stare at each other. They wait. And then they look at me. Everybody does. I guess it's all pretty clear.

I don't feel scared. After all, I have the pistol now.

"Don't worry," our father says. "He'll not do any such thing after he's been with me awhile. He won't dare."

"Those clothes cost a lot of money."

Our father looks down at himself again. "I can see that."

"It'll take more than a batch of knitting to pay for them. And I don't go along much with wife beatings."

"Discipline. And self-discipline. He'll learn it in a hurry when he's with me."

Our father is taking the jacket off and then the vest. Everybody's looking at him, so I run again. But this is different. I've already found out where not to go. I go out, around the house, and then right back and in a window.

As soon as he notices I'm gone, our father yells, "Don't let him get away."

As I hoped, everybody rushes after me. I hear our father jump on his horse. I hear the car door open. The doctor is checking for me in his car. I hear my sister telling Mister Boots to sit down, and I hear that he doesn't obey her, which is very unhorselike for a trusting horse in love, who'd jump off a cliff for you. Perhaps he's more man than I think.

I hear everybody get farther and farther away until, finally, everything's quiet. They're all off someplace. Even Boots. Nobody thinks to look back in the house.

Now's my chance to check for false bottoms. First I go to Mother's cedar chest. It's the most logical. I make a lot of holes in the bottom of it with a kitchen knife and a screwdriver, and it's just a regular bottom. Then I make holes in the bottoms of all of Mother's drawers. Even her yarn baskets. I ruin them all. Our father will say how it's just exactly like me—if he ever finds out.

Pretty soon I hear somebody coming back. I'm still in Mother's room. I roll under the bed and listen. It's Mister Boots and my sister. If they're the ones who find me, it won't be so bad. Especially Boots. I can always talk to him. It's the horse in him that makes him listen.

I might have to stay here all night. I can do that. I can think about throwing fire and going to Los Angeles. I want to so much I start breathing hard, which I should stop or they'll hear me, especially Boots. (He might know about me being here anyway, and not say.) To make myself calm down, I study my hands. I like how stringy and square and brown they are. I think how Mister Boots talked about hands. "The joy of them," he said.

Then I rest my cheek on my hands and listen to my sister and Mister Boots. They're not talking about me or where I might have gone off to. Boots is just talking the way he always does. "The glance of a horse is two separate worlds."

My sister whispers, so all I can hear is, "Something, something, Moonlight." She's loving everything he says, no matter what it is.

I roll over. Right on the pistol. I forgot I had it. I take it out and put it on my stomach. I think about how you have to cock it first. I don't want to forget that. I don't want to shoot anybody—unless I have to. Not anybody here. I need all these people. I even need our father.

Now Boots and my sister come into Mother's room. (All I see is feet.) Boots is saying, ". . . center of gravity. What keeps human beings upright."

My sister says, "That night you were the most mystical magical wonderful thing I ever saw. You were as if made of moonbeams."

"Would you tell me if I should say things in a different way? In order to be a man, I mean. I could change."

"Never. Ever."

"I'm not really like a man."

"That's why I love you."

They're kissing now—or nuzzling—slurping at each other, anyway.

He says, "To think I once thought the round pen was the center of the world, while all the time it was here with you."

Slurp, slurp, slurp—kiss, kiss.

I guess it's kiss, but I'll bet neither one of them knows much about kissing. I may not know from experience, but I know more about all that than my sister. She never found out anything unless from some book or other, and there's no book I ever heard of about "How to Kiss," or I'd have read it myself and long before she ever did.

Then they sit on the bed!

For heaven's sake!

The springs dip down so far they actually touch my face and my stomach. I squinch over to a better spot. Don't they remember Mother died right next to this very bed and not so long ago?

"Do you . . . love?" she says. She's too shy to put the "me" on the end of it.

"As if my meadow," Mister Boots says. "As if my shady tree. You and I, we'd stand, tail to head and head to tail, and swish away each other's flies. We'd drink from the same bucket. If you were gone, I would wait at the gate forever."

Can't he just say "I love you" like everybody else would?

My sister says, "Hold me." I never thought she'd be so bold. First she's supposed to ask him, what are his intentions?

What *are* his intentions, anyway? Why doesn't my sister ask? I'll bet she doesn't care. With Mother gone, I'm the only one around to see that things are done properly. I won't be able to if I go off with our father.

I'm looking up at the bedsprings—right next to my nose. The mattress is light blue. Faded. The springs are rusty. They squeak with the two of them up there.

I don't know what to do. I just keep looking up at the faded blue with rusty marks on it. . . .

And I find the money.

chapter five

I hear the doctor and our father come clattering back. Both of them pound their heels down hard on the porch as they come in, as if they're still angry. That gives Mister Boots and my sister plenty of warning to get out of Mother's room.

Then our father comes into Mother's room and changes his clothes practically right in front of me, except (again) I don't see anything but feet. He gives the clothes back to the doctor. I hear the doctor crank his car, and then I hear him putt-putt-putt away.

Everybody sits down and has coffee and everybody wonders where I could be. Then our father notices the gun isn't under the chair cushion. First he wonders where it got to. Then says, "For sure it's that undisciplined child has it. I don't trust him as far as I can spit." He says it about a dozen times and half a dozen different ways.

The three of them keep on talking about me. Now our father's trying to convince everybody I should go with him. Of course nothing of what he says makes any sense to my sister because she's only thinking that one single thought about me. She doesn't argue, she just says, "He can't go." But she keeps saying "he," so everything is fine.

Finer than fine. I have the gun and I have a lot of money—four bundles of it—and my sister isn't telling on me. I could walk right out to them and I'd be in charge of every single thing and nobody would know it but me.

I put the pistol up there with the money. I climb out Mother's window so it'll look as if I came from outside. I roll in the garden dirt—no special reason—I guess to make them think I come from some odd place out here. I come in by the front door. I walk like I'm in charge of everything, which I am.

I was hoping everybody could tell, but, first thing, our father grabs me by the ankles and flips me upside down, quick as could be, shakes me, and then feels me all over (not the important place).

Mister Boots is looking vicious again.

Our father says, "So! Where is it?"

Why should I stoop to answer? I'm the one who knows everything and has everything.

"I expect that pistol to be back on that table in five minutes, or else."

"It'll take . . . umm . . . three days." I'd better be careful, or I'll get the giggles again.

Even though I'm all dirty from rolling in the garden, my sister comes and hugs me. She's changed in every single way there is. This is a real hug, too. Maybe she doesn't want me to go with our father because she really likes me and wants to look after me just like I want to look after her. I always used to think of my sister not only as shy and scared and ignorant, but as younger than me. Now she seems about the same age.

She and Mister Boots both look kind of rumpled, and her blouse is buttoned up all wrong. That with the buttons doesn't seem at all to be a horsey thing for Mister Boots to have done. That's pure man.

My sister says, "It would be best, you know. We won't watch you go get it."

"The hell we won't!"

My sister is still hugging me as if she wanted to keep me away from our father.

(If I do go get the gun, how come our father doesn't think I'll shoot him with it right away?)

Mister Boots says, "He is being who he is."

Our father looks disgusted. "Straight from the horse's mouth." Why did he put it like that?

I twist away from my sister. It's a lot easier than getting away from our father. Of course this was a hug, not a clutch. I don't run, I just stand there.

Our father takes some metal rings out of his pocket. They're handcuffs, except I don't know this until he snaps them on me and laughs his crazy laugh. He goes on laughing much too long, as if he wants to show what a jolly person he is and how this is just a joke. Then he throws the key way up almost to the ceiling and catches it in his mouth and pretends to chew. "Yum," he says. I don't know where the key really went.

I hadn't noticed until now how graceful his hands are—fat, but graceful even so. They make me think of birds' wings. I'm upset, but I notice. Or maybe I notice because I'm upset.

He says, "Maybe it's my turn to bite you. How'd you like that? Did you ever hear of 'Do unto others'?"

"You already did bite me."

"Bullshit."

My sister flinches when he says that. She doesn't know, even now, what people always say, but with our father around, she soon will.

I pull on the cuffs so hard I hurt my wrists. All of a sudden I realize I'm trapped. I want to reach out. I want to hold things. I can't breathe. I can't think. I hear myself yell, and I didn't even mean to. I kick out at nothing. I'm going crazy. I know I am.

And then I do go crazy. I guess I do. For a minute it's as if here's Moonlight Blue, all hazy . . . right in front of me, the river horse . . . white in the moonlight . . . the sound of hooves, which is the sound of my heart.

Then I'm not just yelling out one big shriek like I like to do to scare people, I'm yelling and yelling and crying at the same time. I wonder if I'm doing it on purpose as a good idea to do. But I don't know if I can stop or not. All of a sudden I'm on the floor, banging my head on Mother's little hooked rug.

My sister goes down on the floor with me and holds me tight so I can't kick or bang my head anymore.

And then I throw up. Right on Mother's rug. That, for sure, I hadn't planned on doing.

I see our father leaning over me. He's taking up all my ceiling. He's raising his hands as if to say, Oh, for heaven's sake.

Then I pass out. Or maybe I just forgot everything right after. That happened to me once when I fell off a horse. All of a sudden I was on the ground, and now, all of a sudden, here's me, on the couch instead of Boots, a damp cloth on my head and no handcuffs anymore. My sister is kneeling on the floor cleaning up Mother's rug. And Boots is sitting beside me on the stool, wiping me off just as tender as could be. He's saying, "Easy now. Sweet boy." I like being called sweet.

Our father is saying, "But what about the pistol? What about that?"

My sister says, "I'll see to it. Don't worry."

And I'm thinking: Well, that was one way to get things done I hadn't ever thought about before, but I'm exhausted. I'm not sure I'd ever want to do that again.

I wish I had turned into a bird instead of all this, and flown away like my sister said I maybe did. I guess I was just about scared enough to have that happen, but it didn't, which is not a good sign for me ever getting to be a bird. I guess it's good I didn't; I'd never have been able to fly with my wings cuffed together like that.

Afterward, when everything's all calmed down, we have iced tea and my sister sits on the couch and holds me on her lap, which never happened before that I can remember. Of course I never wanted her to before. I wouldn't have let her if she'd tried.

Our father says (mostly to my sister), "It's criminal to leave a boy out here doing nothing. Look at him." He reaches over and circles my wrist with his sweaty thumb and forefinger. "No decent food, no decent clothes, no exercise. '*Mens sana in corpore sano,*' I always say. Now a girl would be different, but a boy has to get out of here. If you had any sense you'd see that. What can his future be, stuck way out here? And you, too, knitting your life away? Even Mister Boots here. Does he do anything at all?"

My sister must know that these are very good questions. She doesn't say a word because there isn't anything to say.

"I suppose you think this boy'll go off someday and do something? Well, not unless you let him come along with me." Then, "Women! Always trying to keep everybody safe. There is no safe!"

"Not me," I say. "I don't want to be safe." But nobody is listening.

chapter six

We get to relax and breathe the next morning when our father rides to town (for cigars, and new clothes for me, and something about Mother at the undertaker's, too). I'll bet that horse can get there in no time.

I thought I'd finally have a chance to do something of my own, but Jocelyn talks to me almost the whole time he's gone. I know better than to say one single thing; that just makes people talk more. I go, mm-hmm, mm-hmm.

In a way it's nice. We sit on the couch, and she puts her arm around me, and I put my head on her shoulder. A cross-breeze comes in the kitchen window and blows out through here and on out the screen door. It's one of those days when the sage smells really strong. It almost makes me cry to be so cozy, but I'm tired of all this talk, talk, talk.

"Do you want to be handcuffed again, for heaven's sake? When he was here before, Mother and I did all the dirty work without a minute's rest. If we wanted any money for ourselves, we had to knit. He thinks it's good for people to grow up hardworking, like he did. But . . . Oh dear, I don't know what to do. You know as well as I do you can't go. You just can't! You can't! That's all there is to it."

"I'm not deaf."

She quiets down, and in a bit I actually fall asleep leaning on her shoulder. I don't know how long I sleep, but she lets me stay. (This is a whole new thing—as everything is these days.) I don't wake up until our father comes back. With clothes for me. And shoes!

I've already listened to just about all the talk I can stand for one day, but next thing our father is taking me out by myself, too. Not for a talk (I certainly don't need to be convinced of anything), but to work on tricks. He wants me to get started being his helper.

First thing, our father shows me how to throw fire. It's probably a sort of bribe to get me to want to go with him even more than I already do. But you can't just go off and throw fire whenever you feel like it. It's tricky. You have to be prepared, and you have to use special paper. That's a big disappointment. I think about how Mother said not to believe in magic. Maybe she was right. Throwing fire is just regular once you know how.

Then he shows me about the magic wand and scarves and flowers, and then about other things where you have to stand a certain way, like sideways—even your hands sideways. He tells me how I have to practice all the time to keep my fingers nimble.

He says "Butterfingers" when I drop things, but I'm surprised he doesn't get disgusted with me. All of a sudden he's patient. He said he never loses his temper; that's not true, he did lots of times, but he doesn't now. He says "Good boy" a couple of times, and gives me a man-to-man punch on the shoulder.

Then he tells me he has a nice surprise for me if I practice—something he got for me in town—something I'll like. I wonder if I will.

And then, after all this getting talked at in the morning and taught things all afternoon, right after beans, Mister Boots . . . even Mister Boots takes me out to talk to me. I never had a day like this before.

He wants to go out a ways because it's his first time really away from the house, so we walk down by the irrigation ditch where the grass is long and juicy. Mister Boots likes it there even though, in his present form, he won't be eating any of it. We sit on it instead—at first almost on a killdeer nest. Boots sees the mother bird doing the broken-wing trick to make us come after her, and then he sees the nest and we move a bit farther down. I lie back and look at the moon coming up from behind the mountains and get ready for a lot of his usual nonsense. His voice is soft and

breathy, and he speaks thoughtfully, slowly, like he's thinking hard, and I guess he is.

"I want to say it properly," he says.

His words make me sleepy—in a nice way. They make
me look around at the hills and the mountains, and then
closer in, at blades of grass.

We watch the moon come up till it shines on Mister
Boots so you can almost see Moonlight Blue underneath his
humanness—his face, so pale, his mane blowing. I'm glad
Jocelyn didn't let our father cut it.

"Your sister says I should convince you, but convincing
doesn't convince. If you need to make a mistake, you should
make it. But your sister said to try."

"You always try. But I need to ask you something. It's
important. I need to know your intentions."

"What intentions?"

"We don't just . . . you know human beings don't . . . well,
stand . . . mount and then wander off and then mount somebody else. I mean what are you going to do about my sister?"

"Love her. Isn't that enough? Is that enough?"

"No."

And then I tell him all about marriage, which makes
him thoughtful and sad (not that he doesn't look thoughtful and sad all the time anyway).

"I was told of it, but no one ever told me as well as you
do now."

"You have to stay with her till death do you part. You have to tell her that, and you have to make money."

"Ah," he says, "money. I'm not qualified for that, but I do know loving."

He looks so sad, I almost tell him how I found the money, and that I'll give him half, or all of it if he needs it, but then I think I won't tell quite yet. I might need that money for something special. What if I have to buy Moonlight Blue from the glue-factory people? And I don't even know how much money there is.

Then he says another Mister Boots kind of thing. "Listen," he says. "Listen."

But there's hardly a sound. The wind has died down and the meadow larks are gone; the ditch water is stagnant and still.

"There's nothing."

"That's it. There's nothing. Listen."

First thing the next morning, our father gets me out of bed, which never happened around here before. Since when did anybody care? I get up pretty early on my own, but this is even earlier. I know he's doing it on purpose to teach me a lesson of some sort, though what kind of a lesson is it if I already always get up early? I like dawn. It's my favorite time.

He has me sit up on the kitchen table and cuts my hair

into a real boy's haircut. Better than the haircuts my sister gives me, and he has clippers, which we don't. (They're probably horse clippers for his fancy horse.) It takes a long time. I itch from sitting, and I itch from the hair bits all over me. Our father doesn't let me wash off. After the haircut he sets me to practicing my finger exercises and card shuffling.

Every so often I have this thought in the back of my mind (like when I thought about owning a car): I wonder if a woman can get to be a magician. I've never known a woman to do much more than the things Jocelyn and Mother did. Mostly I don't let myself think about it because, who knows, I might just stay like this—maybe never have to get breasts and all that. Besides, being ten lasts a whole year.

The next morning, first thing, our father goes out to water his horse and give it some grain and it's gone, halter unbuckled, just hanging there. Our father's saddle and saddlebags are neatly slung over the porch rail. I'm surprised this didn't happen earlier. Of course Mister Boots gets around a lot better now.

Our father stamps up and down, muttering to himself about what a valuable horse it is.

He checks for hoofprints, wanders all over in big circles shading his eyes, comes in and slams the screen door, and then opens it just so he can slam it again. He glares around at everything.

But that poor horse stood there a good bit of three days, without a rubdown (except by me) nor a chance to roll in any good dust. We don't have a corral to put him in, but we could have hobbled him with a soft rope or somebody's belt and kept an eye on him so he didn't hop too far. Or we could have asked the neighbors to let him go out in their pastures with their horses.

All of us three know who did it, but our father thinks . . . not only thinks, he *knows* it's me. I wish it had been. I should have done it first thing. I just wasn't paying attention.

"That was a valuable horse," our father says—for about the sixteenth time.

"I did that." I'm glad to take the blame. It would have been a good thing to do.

Except then Boots says, "He didn't."

"Yes I did. How'm I ever going to learn self-discipline if I don't own up?"

"But you didn't."

"It's all right," I say. "Our father knows I did it."

"Damn tootin'."

Our father grabs me by my ear and pushes me outside and around the back, where he pulls up a tomato stake. That's going to break. It's too dry. So then he takes off his belt. At least he holds it by the buckle.

"You've been itching for this ever since I got here."

Boots is right behind us, as fast as if his legs were all well. And then it happens again, except, again, I don't get to see it. I wanted to so badly, but Boots is behind me. I only see our father instead.

First there's something big that cuts off the sun and shades both our father and me. Something that makes our father stare, blinking, right up where the sun had been. There's the sound of hooves again. Dust flies up. There's a swish of black mane at the corner of my eye. . . .

Our father drops the belt and goes down on his knees. I turn around and here's Mister Boots already as himself—perfectly ordinary, skinny old Boots, out of breath, but looking just like himself: dignified and sad. We watch the dust settle—all of us breathing hard.

Then our father comes back to normal, gets up, and puts his belt around his paunch. "I could use that trick," he says. His voice is only a little bit shaky. "I've never seen that done. I know it's your secret, but I'll pay and I'll give you credit and a percentage every time I use it. Or you can come along with us, me and my son here. Is Boots your first name or last name or nickname? As a stage name it won't do."

Doesn't our father see who Boots is even yet?

"How about calling yourself White Lightning? That

would fit with the act, but, well . . . I have to admit you shook me up a bit."

Boots, obedient horse again, speaks as prey to predator. "Boots is my regular name, but if you need me to, I'll change it."

Sometimes it seems he's been too "broke" to be a person.

My sister changes her tactics about me.

We go back in and sit as we usually do: our father, in the big soft chair; Mister Boots and my sister on the couch, touching knees. I'll have to keep an eye on them. Touching knees is all right, but no hanky-panky.

My sister says, "How about if we all go? I won't let Bobby go off alone with you, and that's that. If . . ." She hesitates and then says, ". . . he. If he goes, we all go. We'll follow along behind if you won't let us travel with you."

"All of you?" Our father leans back so his stomach sticks out even more. "What a mess!" He says "Still" a few times. And "Well" a few more, and then he gets all dreamy again and smiles a little secret smile, not the usual one with the big teeth. "White Lightning," he says, talking to himself. "Well now, Mister Boots, if you'll do that illusion of yours, I'll take you all along. You don't even have to tell me how you do it. I'll take you, that is, if you let me cut your hair, like I did the boy's."

Jocelyn jumps up and starts with all those, No, no, no's again. "You can't. It doesn't work that way."

"What is he, like Samson?"

"Sort of."

"Bullshit, if he comes with us, I cut his hair. That's all there is to it. It all comes back to discipline."

"He could tie it up in a . . . ponytail, but he can't cut it."

I'm thinking, Why not? Except she's right; he wouldn't look near as nice as a horse without his wild black mane. And for sure my sister doesn't care what he looks like as a person. I'll bet when she looks at him, she always sees Moonlight Blue.

"And Mister Boots, if you interfere with my disciplining of this boy all the time, he'll end up becoming a criminal. Look at me. You think I wasn't whipped? It's just like with horses. 'The more you beat 'em the better they be.' Ever heard that? It's not only about dogs and women and walnut trees."

Boots throws his head again, up and down, and it's not a yes. The reins are too tight, and he wants to shake the whole idea out of his head.

"I presume that's a yes."

(Boots could take his shirt off and show his back—his whole body actually. Of course that will just be one more proof to our father of how well whipping works, because Boots is a nice creature, horse or man.)

Our father gets his dreamy look again. "Lassiter and Son," he says. "And Magical Horse."

I wonder if Boots can change himself when he feels like it.

But has everybody forgotten our father's horse is missing? I guess they have. I'd like to get out of here, so I say, "How about if I go get your horse for you? Since it's all my fault. I know every single place where a horse might want to be."

I guess our father's afraid I'll never come back, except why would I not when I want to go with him so badly? Or maybe our father thinks I'll find the horse and then go off and sell him, which would be a good idea, but I could never get away with it around these small towns. Everybody would know. And anyway, I have a lot of money already.

But instead of me, it's our father who goes out on one of the neighbors' horses. He doesn't ask if he can borrow one any more than I do. It's bad, though, because, even though he goes out rattling a pail of grain, Rusty is the only horse that will let him catch her. She's much too small for a man his size. I could have caught any of them just by standing still, not looking at them. They all come to me.

While he's gone my sister goes on with her knitting. I still haven't told her I found the money, so she probably thinks she has to keep at it.

Our father sweats up poor little Rusty and himself and doesn't find his horse. I knew he wouldn't.

"I guarantee I can find him. And I'm not going to run away. Why would I, since I want to go with you?"

He's all hot and bothered. I can see he wants to say his favorite bad words, but instead he says, "All right, all right, all right."

(Houdie, that's his horse's name. It's a silly name for such a fancy horse. Except his real name is Houdini's Escape.)

"So what'll you give me when I bring him back safe and sound?"

"A spanking if you don't, that's what. And you'd better come back, toot sweet. And while you're at it, don't forget to bring back the pistol."

I'm so glad to get out of there and off by myself I think maybe I really will run away. I run out shouting "Yay, yay" and "Yes, yes, yes, yes," yelling like I do when I want to scare people.

I get to go get a horse that isn't old and ordinary. I don't have to use grain or carrots and go out with a halter hidden behind my back. (Since our father's horse doesn't know me, I do bring a lead rope for bringing him home just in case.)

I'll need a horse. (Not Rusty. She's too tired.) I walk out and around like I do and then stand still. Pretty soon every horse gets curious about what I'm doing there. They know me and come to greet me. They know I'll take them through the gate and we'll go have fun. We usually go where it's nice and grassy, and I always let them graze in juicy new fresh spots.

I really do know where our father's horse is. I like that place myself. There's a little stream that comes down from the mountains. That stream feeds the little pond they've dammed off at the neighboring ranch. Once you're far enough up, there's blackberry bushes. The berries taste better than those from any other place. I always brought some back to Mother.

Tears come—because of thinking about Mother—and then, right after I get over one batch, along comes another batch, because if I go off with our father, maybe I won't ever be here again, and this is one of my favorite places.

I jump off and let the horse go. She'll just eat this good grass for a while and then go back to her herd.

I sit on the bank of the creek. It's just a teeny-weeny little creek, but it's nice and gurgly. I look around at the willows and aspen and listen. There's raven sounds—jays, too. I'm not in a hurry because I want our father to worry about how maybe I'm gone for good.

I sit and just look, and pretty soon here comes Houdie, curious as a horse. They always want to know what's going on, as who wouldn't? And since I'm all hunkered down here in a lump, not at all threatening, he comes right up to me to see what I am. I don't move at all. I hold my breath and use my magic. It's still good. Finally I reach out and let him blow on my hand, and then I blow on his nose. Then I stroke him, and we get to be friends. I still don't get up. I'm in no more of a hurry than he is.

(How will we keep Mister Boots from letting Houdie go again? That's the one main thing he likes to do. When his legs get well, it'll be even worse. Of course the doctor said they'd never heal completely, which is a good thing for anybody who wants to keep their animals. We'd better get an automobile. Wouldn't that be something! I probably have enough money for it all by myself.)

chapter seven

Little by little our father is getting everybody packed up.
He doesn't trust any of us to do it properly. Not even our
own stuff. Even when we pack something up nice and neat,
he unpacks it and does it over. It's true, he can get twice as
much stuff into a box as we can—he's had a lot of practice—
but why don't we get to practice? This way we'll never learn.

We have to travel light, because of all his magic things,
though most of his stuff is in storage down in Sylmar.
That's a place just north of Los Angeles.

He paints a big yellow stripe on everything that doesn't
already have one—even Jocelyn's purse and knitting basket,
so we and everybody can see, real fast, what belongs to us. I
paint a yellow stripe across my forehead and that just makes
them mad and I have to get washed with turpentine.

Of course during all this packing is when our father dis-
covers the ruined drawers in Mother's room and the ruined
bottom of Mother's cedar chest.

This time, instead of coming to me with a switch or

taking off his belt, he goes to Mister Boots and brings him into Mother's room—which is our father's room now. (He doesn't know what he's sleeping on top of.)

"Mister Boots, just look at all this. You have to let me do what needs to be done. And how do you suggest I get that pistol back? You know it's not safe for a boy to have that."

Our father hasn't figured out yet how Boots just plain hates for any creature to get whipped—even a little tiny bit of a switching to a tiny little creature.

Boots says, "He brought you back Houdie. That's a kindness." Then, "There are better ways."

"Well I don't know any."

At least I don't get whipped.

Our father not only won't let me take any of my favorite things, but not any of my old clothes. Only these new things he bought in town. They match my new boy hair-cut: two pairs of heavy corduroy knickers, white shirts and plaid shirts, a bow tie, a tweed cap, striped pajamas. And shoes! Our father got them much too big, so there's room to grow. He says I have to wear them from now on. He says we're going off to where people are civilized, not like around here.

"But can't I have just one single little box of things for myself? Please? Just one little one? That locks?" (If he doesn't say yes, what will I do with the pistol and the money? You can't wear things like that on you all the time.) "Well, what about Jocelyn's knitting then? It's bulky. Does she get to take all that?"

It's yes to her and no to me—he says because I'm a boy and boys don't need a lot of things like girls do. Boys travel light and get along with practically nothing. But he's the one with the most stuff of any of us, and he hasn't even got all of it yet. And that pink turban has a great big padded box all its own.

So the big surprise our father got for me in town is—for heaven's sake—a baseball and mitt. I'm supposed to bring those along instead of a little box of my own special secret things!

He gives them to me when he sees how I'm practicing my quarters-out-of-ears. He says my fingers are small, but I'm dexterous for my age (which, as far as I know, nobody has told him what that is). I even surprise myself. Quarters are coming out of everywhere. That's one trick you can do anywhere as long as you have a quarter. Maybe I can get rich asking people for quarters. Except I'm already rich. I wish everybody would go away so I'd have a chance to get the money out from under our father's bed and count it.

I show Jocelyn how good I am at quarters, but she gives me one of those smirky smiles. She thinks no good will come of any of this.

"But don't you want adventures? Our father's right you know; nothing's going to happen here."

"Moonlight Blue is enough of something happening for me. I'd rather just be here with him."

"But you know exactly what to do to stop this."

"First of all, our father won't believe us without you completely naked. He's thought you were a boy from the very first. He got it into his head all by himself, and he was so delighted that he finally had a boy who didn't die at birth that Mother didn't dare tell him the truth. Mother was afraid I'd say something. She said she didn't know what he was capable of. For a while he was good to her because of you being a boy. I remember flowers all the time. I hate to think what will happen when he finds out."

"There isn't going to be a when."

I think even if things do turn out badly, it'll be good for all of us to get out of here. I say, "I was born to travel," though this is the first I've thought that.

My sister says, "Pooh."

The very next day our father gets me up before dawn; it's to go—I can't believe it—fishing! He's taking time out from packing and repairing his old magic boxes. He thinks this is something I must have always wanted to do, especially with him. A boy and his dad.

I can't think of anything I'd rather not do than go

fishing. I hate all the things where you have to sit. But most of all I don't want to be off alone with our father even though it's a beautiful morning, the mountains turning purple, and there's pink outlining the tops of the highest. Birds are waking up. I love this time of day, but I wish I was alone. Even though we get along all right when he teaches me magic, I don't trust him.

We go off without any breakfast because our father thinks that will be good discipline for me.

"Even if you're sick or starving, the show must go on. Might as well practice that."

Of course the more he likes me, the more I might get to drive the trotter someday. So while we do the fishing thing, I don't talk because, the way I feel, I'll surely say something he'll think is sassy.

He doesn't talk either. He's smoking a cigar and humming. He sounds a lot better than when Boots is trying to sing, but I'd rather it was Boots, grunting out what he thinks is a tune instead of our father's . . . they call that "baritone." He sounds as if he can really sing, then, all of a sudden, it's "Danny Boy," loud and clear and beautiful. Kind of fits with the sunrise.

After a long while he says, "Isn't this cozy?"

My stomach growls back at him.

We listen to the birds and pretty soon he says, "You have to admit, a boy of your sort needs a lot of looking after."

Sit and sit.

"Put all that energy of yours into useful projects."

Growl, growl goes my stomach, and tweet go the birds.

All of a sudden he says, "Have a puff," and hands me his cigar. And I do and then I cough. "If you're a chip off the old block, you'll get to like it one of these days."

Mister Boots hates that cigar smell. Just thinking *Boots* makes me see things in a different way. I lie back on the creek bank and see the sky through a screen of weeds. That's the horse way.

But there's somebody out there, way, way off. I lift my head out of the weeds, and it's Boots. I recognize him from the hat he always wears—Jocelyn's old gardening hat—a ladylike kind of hat for a man, but Boots doesn't mind. He's staying pretty far away, and he's riding a horse! With his bad legs, he can't come out here without riding. He's doing it for my sake, that's what. I see our father sees him, too.

Wouldn't it be funny if Boots changed while he was riding, so one horse was plopped on top of another? I laugh out loud.

"You giggle at nothing just like a girl. You'll scare the fish away."

Pretty soon I'm so hungry I can't stand it. I actually get a stomachache. After all, I'm a growing boy.

Finally we head back, but before we go in, our father says he needs to check on how I throw a ball, and then he's upset by the way I do it. He says I throw like a girl. He says I can't eat until I throw properly. It takes a half an hour's worth of more starving, but I finally do it—throw a couple of times like a boy. I thought maybe I never would be able to, being what I am. I wonder what it means about me that I finally got so I can do it.

Right after what might be called breakfast, I help my sister do the dishes, which I normally don't. Mister Boots does that a lot, though our father thinks it's not a good thing for a man or boy to do, so I'm doing it for lots of good reasons, though it would be easy to get out of.

"Jocelyn, I want you to teach me how to knit—right now, right after dishes."

"Do you think that's wise?"

"Please, please, pleeeease! I'll help with the dishes every single time if you'll teach me. I can practice it while you sew me up the costume for the show."

"I don't think you should."

"Well, since you think I shouldn't knit, but I think you ought to marry Mister Boots before something bad happens, then we're even."

"Our father thinks we're already married, so everything is fine. Besides, how would we do it? I, Moonlight Blue, take thee . . . or, I, Boots . . . ? And I think you have to have papers and things to prove you're you. Birth certificates and such. Besides, I don't care one way or the other."

"Where were you brought up?" Which is what Mother used to say all the time.

"This is nothing like any other relationship in the whole world. Boots isn't a man. He won't run off like our father always does. And you'd better watch out; our father might run off again. What if he did it when we were stuck out in the middle of nowhere? Then where would we be?"

"We're out in the middle of nowhere already."

Jocelyn does start me knitting right after we finish the dishes. I think she wants to see what will happen as much as I do. It's to be a scarf for Mister Boots. She lets me pick the color, which is navy blue.

She starts me up and sets me out on the porch steps. For the first time in my life I feel like a girl. So this is how Mother and Jocelyn felt all day long and on into the night. My knitting doesn't look at all like anything she and Mother ever did. It's not easy. I was sorry for them before, but now, what with dropping stitches and all, I'm even sorrier.

We're waiting to see what our father's going to say, but he fools us. He looks at me hard and long, but he doesn't say anything. Then he gets busy repairing those old broken magic boxes. And pretty soon he comes out on the porch and sits beside me to paint new golden curlicues on them.

"Throws a ball like a girl, but knits like a boy," he says.

Pretty soon I hear from the tone of our father's voice

that he's finally come around to what he wanted to say when he first came out here on the porch.

"You'll inherit all these valuable things; everything I own will be yours. All I ask is that you keep the show on the road. That's all I'll ever ask, that you learn the business and keep the name Robert Lassiter in the public eye. We're on the same team, you know. The magic makers against everybody else."

Maybe this is a good thing. I'm the son and heir. Robert Lassiter the second. Why not?

I say, "I will. I'll do it."

He reaches down, pulls my hand away from my knitting (I drop a half a line of stitches), and makes me shake hands—man to man.

It takes me ten minutes to get back to where I was. I'm not going to give up. I want Boots to have this scarf.

So we sit awhile doing what we're doing, and then our father says if I give him back the pistol, he'll get me a BB gun—a rifle. I think having a real grown-up person's pistol is better.

"I'll teach you how to shoot. We'll shoot together."

Yeah, I know, just like we fished—sit out in the woods without any breakfast waiting for something to walk by and get shot.

"So, that's settled, then, all of us going. It might work out. You'll like the train. I always did like trains. First there's a hundred miles of the narrow gage. Then we have to change to the full-sized one. You're going to like them both."

Then he says we've got to board up the windows. This is getting scary. What will be here to come back to? I start thinking about Mother again. Mother wouldn't like this at all. She loved this place just as much as I do.

I have to go somewhere. I get up. I throw down the knitting and give this yell, which I didn't even mean to. Our father spills his paint, and I hear Jocelyn, way inside the house, drop something that breaks.

I give a couple of big jumps (I need to after so much sitting), then I run off. Every other step is as if saying Mother. Mother, step, Mother, step, Mother, Mother, Mother, step . . . Sometimes I have to realize all over again that she's really dead.

Without thinking, I end up by my tree, walking and running all the way. Nobody comes after me. I'll have to walk all the way back, too. I don't care. It's for Mother.

I shout a couple more shouts. Out here it doesn't matter. I lie down with my head on a big rough root. I make myself as flat as possible so nobody can see me unless they're right on top of me, and I look around at all the mountain peaks. I recognize every single lump and hump and pinnacle in every direction. I've looked at them since I first could look. I could draw them all with my eyes shut.

I suck at the inside of my elbow. Better than a thumb, clean and soft, and not so babyish. I think about Mother. I think, again, how the breeze on my cheek is her touch. I cry some. Until there's no more tears. Then I just lie and look up. I may spend the night here.

All of a sudden, there's something snuffling at me—wet, sloppy, warm. . . . I guess I went to sleep. I sit up fast, but it's just my friend Houdie. Boots has let him go again. I'll bet I'll be blamed for it even though I wasn't there. I'll have a ride home though. Maybe Boots whispered in Houdie's ear, in some kind of horse talk, that he should come out here and bring me home.

So what's the best thing to do? Give him a yell and a slap on the rump and make him run off into the hills while he has the chance? Or bring him on home with me for Boots to let him go again some other time?

Our father goes to town again to order a wagon to take us and all our stuff to the train; Boots and my sister go off down the road a ways to sit by the irrigation ditch and be alone; so I finally have a chance to count the money. It's five hundred and fifty-eight dollars. I *am* rich. I take the heavy cardboard box that has my new clothes packed in it and I unpack it and make a false bottom. I don't think our father will expect that on an ordinary cardboard box. I put in the money and the pistol and one horseshoe and one rabbit's foot. I take forty dollars to have on me in case of emergencies. I might need to help Jocelyn or Mister Boots in a hurry.

The day before we leave, our father tries to get Boots to do his horse trick. He works on him half the morning. Boots just shakes his head. (By now he knows how to do it to mean no.) "I never met a man so . . . Are you crazy or just stupid?" He says, "Be reasonable," a dozen times. "I can't pay you if you won't work." Then, "Do I have to start to whip the boy to make you do it? I'll do that if I have to."

He turns and gives me a good swat on the bottom for no reason, all the time looking at Boots instead of me.

Boots kicks out, but just an ordinary, human being kind of kick, though who but a horse would think of kicking first?

Our father believes in fighting, and he's good at it, you can tell. He gets two good punches in right away. Boots is already off balance from trying to kick and down he goes in the dust and gets a bloody nose right away. He doesn't even try to get up, and he doesn't change to Moonlight Blue. I wanted him to. I want our side to win.

Boots sits there looking up at us, calm as could be, but I get up and go right at our father. I'm only tall enough to hit his stomach, except I don't land a single blow. He just puts his hand on my forehead, and I can't reach him.

"Boy, I admire your spirit, but you'd better think a little bit about which side your bread is buttered on." He gives me a push so I'm on the ground next to Boots, and then he walks away looking disgusted.

I find a rag for Boots's nose. I tell him, "Don't worry anything at all about money."

"I never do," he says.

But I'm mad at him. I say, "You don't even know what it is."

"I suppose not."

"You ought to find out. You ought to learn things."

I can't read that horse look of his. I could tell if he had his horse ears on him.

chapter eight

I turn out to be the hit of the show! In one way I'm not at all surprised, though in another way I am. I probably have more magic in me than anybody around here. But I'm the big hit partly because I look so much younger than I really am. Our father has taken advantage of it and advertised that I'm only seven. I have to go along with that, though I don't like it. It's hard enough getting all the way up to ten without going backward.

Except I don't understand how I got to be the main attraction, because our father's so good. People love him. Even I love him. The first performance we do changes my mind about everything. It's nothing like our rehearsals. Everything looks exciting, people ooh and aah, and our father is—he actually is—kind of wonderful. Onstage he's not the same person at all. He looks bigger. Not just fatter but taller, too. Now I see what that loud voice of his is for: booming out, deep and like singing. He's all sparkly under the spotlight. Even his hair looks nice and shiny. Even that funny little mustache and goatee, which I always thought were useless . . . even they look good. He's . . . devilish, black and white all over. The only colors are in the scarves and flowers and painted boxes . . . and me in my pink. (Onstage he calls me Pixie. He says, "I'll bring on my magic pixie." He snaps his fingers and here I come. I guess I do look like a pixie. I don't mind that, except for being pink.)

I see Jocelyn look at him just the way I must be looking, her eyes as wide-open as her mouth.

And I see how Mother could have fallen in love and not even cared who he was when he wasn't onstage.

I always thought I didn't want him to be my father, but now I think we're two of a kind: born to travel and born to be onstage and born to make our voices go right out across all the people's heads and out the lobby doors, and on into the street. For a change I'm not thinking "*our* father," I'm thinking "*my* father."

But through the whole train trip down, I was getting angrier and angrier with him telling us all what to do and when to do it, where to sit, who got a window seat and for how long, when we'd eat and what we'd eat. (Oranges are good for us. I, in particular, have to eat them. I like them, but I don't want to *have* to eat them every day.) He made Mister Boots and me carry heavy things while Jocelyn, because she's a girl, only had to carry her knitting. I know, like

Mother said, life isn't fair, but it ought to be a little tiny bit more fair than this.

He kept saying (just to me, not to anybody else), "Sit up. Breathe deeply. Fill your chest with this good country air." (As if I didn't always live in the middle of good country air.) "Don't scuff when you walk." Well, my shoes are too big so I can't help it. But there's no use telling him that. "No excuses!" is another of his favorite things to say. "Do you think there are any excuses in the army?"

We have so much baggage I thought we were never going to get anywhere, but our father's used to moving all this stuff. He was busy and distracted, and he made us keep quiet so we wouldn't, as he kept saying, break his concentration; otherwise it would be our fault if he forgot something important.

He said he'll need us to be quiet before every show, too, so he can compose himself psychically. By the time we got on the train, I was worn out from keeping quiet.

And I got worn out all over again just from how it looked out the train window: a whole other world—black or red volcanic domes and cones; places with a lot of dead trees where there used to be ditches but the water's all taken down south to Los Angeles, where we're going.

Our father was explaining what it all was and how it got that way. I might have liked hearing all that if it hadn't been our father telling it.

Mister Boots and I saw a herd of wild horses, six of them. That was a time when we both had window seats. Boots looked over at me, surprised. The horses ran as the train passed by, tails and manes flying. Boots looked like he'd never thought such a thing could be, or a thing so free, or that it could look so beautiful. Magic passed between us—a different kind of magic. Like we'd seen all the way inside each other. Afterward I could tell he was thinking hard.

(When we started out and my sister saw me for the very first time, head to toe, in my new boy clothes—cap and shoes and all—she covered her face with both hands and gasped. It's like she finally realized. I guess I did, too. But realizing isn't going to change anything. I realized it before with the baseball and mitt and fishing pole.)

Pretty soon our father wants Mister Boots to join the act. I don't know why our father needs Boots, what with me being such a big hit, but he thinks he does, and I'm the one supposed to bring Boots onstage and make him change.

I told our father it won't work, and that Boots doesn't care anything about whether he gets paid, or famous, or if he makes a fool of himself, but our father is so sure he'll do it, he's made a poster about it except with the wrong color horse, pure white all over, mane and everything. (Why does he think Boots is called Boots, for goodness' sake?)

I'm on the poster, too: LASSITER THE MAGIC MAN
AND SON. And, in smaller letters: SEVEN-YEAR-OLD
PRODIGY OF PRESTIDIGITATION.

So I lead Boots in—this skinny, nothing little man. It's
exactly the opposite of when our father's onstage, because
Boots looks smaller and thinner than ever, but people clap
anyway. They think he's going to do something, or else why
would he be out here in front of everybody? I lead him in
with a halter dangling around his human-being neck.

Boots is hobbling, head down and forward. He lets me
lead him because it's me. He says he owes me a lot, but he
says he won't change to Moonlight Blue even for my sake.
As we stand in the wings I tell him, "Do something, anyway. Sing or dance or something. Our father's already mad
enough at you."

"I've been trying."

"I know you have. You always try. You've been doing
most of the hard work, but you know he doesn't care about
anything except what happens onstage."

When we come onstage, Boots looks all around, blinking, blinded by the lights. He shades his eyes as if he's in
the sun. (Our father said you aren't supposed to do that
even if you feel like it.) Nobody is clapping anymore.
Everybody waits.

If I had a pin I'd drop it right now.

Then Boots says, "Stop!" His voice isn't strong. It's as if he's a horse right now—it's blowy, too much air in it. Only the first six or eight rows can hear him. "Stop. Think. These rabbits. These doves. Your horses. We labor beside you at the work of the world."

He bobs his head, horselike as usual. His mane comes loose from its ponytail and swishes back and forth. And there's his bony forehead, bony horse nose. . . .

"Think . . . All your doves and rabbits . . ." As if everybody had them.

But that's all the time our father gives him. He stamps out onstage and grabs him by the halter, twists it tight across his neck, says, "Come on, Dobbin." Our father leans way back and walks a funny duck walk, high knees, swinging his fat hind end. (He can laugh at himself if need be, especially if need be onstage.) The tails of his dress coat swish back and forth and make the waddle even more so. He leads Boots into the wings. He really is choking him. Boots couldn't say anything more if he tried. Our father finds boxes and such to bang around, so there's a nice clatter from backstage, as if he'd thrown Boots against things that fell over. Everybody laughs. Our father's turned it into a clown act. I jump a couple of jumps and yell, "Whoopee!" to help out. Everybody laughs some more. This is turning out to be a good thing.

Even so, and even though our father keeps telling us he

never gets angry, he turns red with holding it in. He's in practice for having the show go on, though. Red as he is, he keeps everything moving the way it's supposed to.

He's so angry he stays red-faced all evening.

Usually, in front of strangers, he's as jolly as can be. He talks to everybody. Tells jokes. Tells about funny things that happened onstage and how cleverly he worked things into the act. Tells about how he met Houdini. Though he doesn't drink much, he loves to go to bars and takes me, too. He introduces me to everybody, "My son, a chip off the old block. Only seven years old and could do the whole act by himself if need be." He keeps me up late just to show me off. We hardly ever get to bed before two in the morning. Especially after we've given a show and are still all excited.

Now he doesn't know what to do with himself. Paces, red-faced, then stops pacing, turns his usual pale again, and stays pale all the rest of the evening.

When I'm just getting ready for bed, he comes for me. "All right," he says. "Don't think you don't need a lesson just as much as Boots does." He walks me out and down the road until there aren't any more streetlamps.

It's a pretty dark night. There's only a little half a moon. First thing, he pulls off all my clothes and I think: Here it comes. I get worried. I don't want to be alone with him way out here when he finds out. Especially not when he's so upset.

But it's too dark and he's not paying attention. What he does find is my rabbit's foot and twenty dollars, which makes him even angrier. In this light he can't tell how much money it is, he just knows it's money. He thinks I stole it.

He really whips me. He uses a leather thong kind of thing—four thongs braided into a handle at one end. It was made exactly for this. I've seen those hanging in the grocery stores, and I guessed it was for children but I wasn't sure.

I didn't do one bad thing—not one single thing. I took care of the doves and the rabbits. I led Boots in just like he said to. Then I was just sitting there reading before getting into bed and at the same time rolling two bits along my fingers, exactly like I'm supposed to do.

I don't cry out. What's the use? I just squeak a little.

He's mad about all the other times when Mister Boots wouldn't let him whip me, though I think he's mainly mad about Boots.

He talks all through it. "Turn over a . . ." *Whip.* ". . . new leaf." *Whip.* "Make a man." *Whip.* "*Man!*" *Whip.* "And hand over that pistol the minute we get back."

"It's back home."

"I don't believe it."

(I wish I could throw fire anytime I feel like it.)

But after a few minutes I start to float above everything, as if I'm watching us down here. It's as if I can see better than I really can: a skinny naked girl (I see that she's a girl just as clear as could be) and a fat man. At first I think I really have turned into a bird, like Jocelyn says I did, but I don't go flying off anywhere, and pretty soon I come back down to myself, which is a big disappointment.

I remember putting my clothes back on and then getting carried, and getting laid on my bed. Gently. I even think he kissed my forehead.

Later here's Jocelyn and Mister Boots sitting by my bed, Boots's arm across her shoulders and my sister's arm around his waist. They're not noticing me at all.

I see I'm in my boy's striped pajamas, but my sister must have undressed me because things seem to be the same. Jocelyn is saying, "Why don't you want to?" and Boots is saying, "Human beings don't do it like that. I'm trying to be one of the good ones."

"Stay Moonlight Blue. I never met a man I liked . . . even a little bit."

I ache all over, and I want somebody to know it. "Hey," I yell, loud enough to make them jump.

Jocelyn gets me water, but when she tries to help me drink, I yell a big "Ouch!" I hurt some, but not as much as I'm pretending.

My sister leans her head next to mine and starts to cry. Mister Boots nibbles at her neck. She turns around to kiss him. I have to yell ouch again to get them to pay attention.

Jocelyn raises me up and I drink, and then she goes to get me broth and crackers.

We're in a hotel. Our father said not a very good one. I don't know why he says that because, though the rooms are small, they're nicer than back home and the beds are not so lumpy and the bathroom is good.

I tell Mister Boots I was scared but I didn't change into anything. "I wanted to fly away, but I couldn't do it. I did float up a little bit, but just a few feet, and then I came right back down. I wanted to turn owl and fly off silently in the dark like they do."

"Human being is better."

(When it comes right down to it, if I'm going to change to anything else at all, it ought to be to a boy.)

The next day I'm really and truly sick—shaky and feverish and wobbly. I don't know why our father whipped me when he's supposed to only do things for the good of the show. But, just like he always complains about *me*, I don't think he was thinking at all.

Thank goodness our father is staying away from us. I get to sit with my sister and go on trying to learn to knit. By now I'm getting good at that, too, just like I'm good at everything else. The scarf for Boots is a little lumpy at the beginning but it's getting better all the time. It'll look good on him when he wears his red sweater. And Jocelyn is knitting a sweater for me the same color as this scarf. "Moonlight navy blue," we call it.

Mostly we don't talk much, and I get to have her read to me. I'm hoping I stay sick a long time. I don't know where she got the money, but on her own, she buys *Anne of Green Gables*, which is a girl's book, and which we'd better not let our father see. He bought a couple of books for me about heroes: baseball heroes, football heroes, army heroes. . . . My sister doesn't want to read those to me. She thinks things have gone too far already.

Our father keeping away from us is a nice rest. He'd probably tell me not to slouch even in bed. He'd say, "Lie straight like a soldier, and keep your toes pointed up."

He goes onstage by himself, but everybody's heard about me and they all want me. Jocelyn was there, and she said they yelled not only for me but for "the magic horse." They think they're cheated unless they get everything that's on the poster. Our father had to get out his old posters, where there's only him. But some of those old posters have a woman on them with fuzzy red hair, and she's dressed in pink with puffed sleeves just like I am, except you can practically see her whole chest.

chapter nine

As soon as I'm a little better our father hires a wagon and a motorcar and takes us out to a tenting place. I slouch all the way, and he doesn't say a single word. I slouch so much I don't even like it myself because I can't see out the window. Not only that, I have to slouch sideways because my bottom still hurts.

This is a funny kind of place. It's full of people like us—all kinds of show people. I like it. I wouldn't mind living here forever. You can hear the creek from our tents. There are big cottonwoods, and you can hear the wind blowing through them. But Jocelyn doesn't like it. I admit it looks kind of ragged. Away from the trees, people have old blankets strung up so as to make more shade. The whole place looks like a bunch of laundry hanging out, and half of it *is* laundry.

Our father is still, mostly, staying away from us. Jocelyn says he told her what he wants me to do. Besides an orange every day, he wants me out in the sun every afternoon for my health, bare to the waist, half an hour front and half an hour back, no more and no less, and I have to have my eyes covered. But because of my whip marks, I'm supposed to do this between the big tent and the middle-sized one, toward the back, and Jocelyn is supposed to sit out in front and keep people away. There's bushes that hide me from the back.

Every now and then I catch a glimpse of our father. He's easy to spot because he wears his turban all the time. Out here he wears it even when he isn't onstage, though he never did that before. Lots of people go around in funny hats or parts of costumes. (There's a clown who wears his big red nose all the time, though the rest of his clothes are just regular.)

We'll have to be careful with Boots here because there's a little pasture with the animals that belong to the people of the camp. Of course horses, but goats and sheep . . . all sorts of things. We don't want Boots to let things go free. We'll get kicked out if that happens and people find out it was us. Besides, a lot of these are performing animals— there's a horse that can count. (That's a lie, like most things around here.) There's a lot of little dogs here that can do all sorts of tricks. When I'm not soaking up sunshine, I watch them get trained. Boots watches, too. At first he worried about them, but then he saw they were having fun.

Jocelyn is worried because some of these people are kind of dark and look to her like gypsies, but Mister Boots says, "I'm a flea-bit gray."

Later Jocelyn asked me, What did I think he meant by that?

A brown person does come—a girl about my age. First she hides at the back, where the bushes are, and watches me when I'm roasting myself in the afternoon sun. First I hear her. I uncover my eyes, but I don't see anybody. Then she creeps out and I put my finger to my lips so she won't make a noise. Jocelyn might hear and make her go away.

"Can we whisper?"

"Come closer then."

First thing she says is she got whipped, too.

"Everybody gets whipped." I say that, though I never got whipped except when our father was around.

"It's always for my own good," she says.

"I get whipped for things I didn't even do."

"Not me. I do lots of bad things, and they don't always find out. Except mostly I didn't know they were bad till after. But sometimes, like if I drop something, I do them by mistake."

"Grown-ups drop things all the time, and nobody whomps them even when they break something or spill things."

"I know that."

"I know you know that."

"I *know*!"

She sits for a while looking at my back, and I go on soaking up sunshine like our father wants me to do.

Then she asks . . . *the* question, "Are you a boy or a girl?"

"Which do you think?"

"Sometimes I think one and sometimes I think the other."

"Have you been watching me?"

"I could find out which you are right now—in half a minute."

I grab myself with both hands so she can't.

"Just wait. I'll get a chance later."

"You won't. I'm fast. Besides, I'm magic."

"I could find out by your name."

"It's Bobby. That's for both girls and boys."

"I'm Rosie. You can't make that into a boy's name."

"I'm a boy."

"You're not."

"I am, too."

"Prove it."

(I'll bet she'd jump if I threw fire. I'll bet she'd jump if I shot my pistol.)

"I'm ten." She says it like she's proud of it.

"That's nothing; I am, too."

Then I see that Jocelyn knows she's here, but she isn't doing anything about it. That's a relief. I should have known she'd be on my side.

I don't care at all that Rosie is one of the brownish people. Besides, they're not gypsies. She's from Mexico, and she
says everybody's brown down there. I like her color better
than mine. She says her father is a circus-horse trainer. She
says Mexicans are the best. Only the Shoshone are better at it.

Rosie says they say if you can kiss your elbow you can
turn into a boy. We both try. I tell her, "Just because I'm
trying doesn't mean I'm a girl. What if I'm a boy that wants
to be a girl? What if it would work that way, too?"

Even though one of my elbows is crooked, and even
though I try really hard, I can't do it.

Lying here before Rosie came, I'd already done just about
all the thinking I could think of to think, but then, after
Rosie, I have a new thought. I think one of these days I'm
going to go out as a girl. Rosie and I could go out together. Rosie is just about my size. She only has two dresses,
and they're awfully dirty and ragged, but I never did mind
dirt like Jocelyn does.

I don't ever want to leave this place. It's much better
than a hotel, and the people are fun. Rosie and I see each
other every day. We found a secret place where we made a
whole village. We used sticks for people and we made houses out of stones and we made roads. The only real thing we
have is one old lead soldier Rosie found. It's the hero. We
take turns with it. Till now I hardly knew there was such a
thing as this kind of playing.

The summer is beginning to be hot, but here by the creek and under these big trees it's cooler. I keep pretending I'm worse off than I really am. I yell ouch even when I'm not hurting. Jocelyn knows that, but she's pretending I'm worse off than I am, too. She likes it because our father keeps away a lot. I especially like it because I've found my first friend who's my own age.

Our father is thinking about a clown suit for Mister Boots. Jocelyn is supposed to sew it up, but she's not sure if she should or not. She thinks our father is doing it on purpose to humiliate Boots. She's upset that Boots isn't upset about it. He's supposed to lope onstage on a hobbyhorse.

"I don't want him made a fool of. I don't want him to be a clown."

I say, "There's nothing wrong with being a clown. Besides, he'd be what you call comic relief."

"I don't want Moonlight Blue to be it."

But then along comes this lady.

By now, since I'm better, our father is coming around a lot more, so that nice rest we were having is over with. He hadn't eaten with us for a while, but now he does all the time. So one mealtime this lady comes, and first thing she calls our father My Dear, and she hugs him and kisses him, then steps back and takes a good look at him and then goes through the whole thing all over again. She gets lipstick all over him.

It's hard to tell if our father is glad to see her or not, but he's surprised. He puts up a good front, though. He has to be an actor for his job, so he can act any way he wants to be. He calls her My Dear, too.

She says, "It's been years."

She has this dead animal around her neck. It has shiny, dark brown, sad eyes. I keep looking at it so much I hardly notice her. It's hot for wearing a fur, but if I had one I'd be wearing it, too. I wonder if she talks to it? I wonder if it was a boy fur or a girl fur back when it was alive?

It isn't till later that I notice—I mean *really* notice—that she has very, very, curly red hair, a lot of it. I know where I've I seen that before!

This lady is just the opposite of Mother, but she acts as if she thinks she's married to our father. Now that Mother's dead I guess it doesn't matter, but they can't both be the real wife.

While she's still hugging and kissing our father, my sister whispers to me, "That's the lady in the old poster. She's a lot fatter now, but I'm pretty sure it's her. That lady had the exact same hair."

She kisses our cheeks and then looks at us longer than feels right. She sees things. She says, "How absolutely perfect, a boy and a girl." She might really mean it, or maybe, unlike our father, she sees what I am right away.

There must be something in our eyes, because she says, "I think you children ought to know right away, your father's been married to me for twenty-five years, and we never divorced." Then she smiles a motherly smile that turns wicked right in the middle of it, and she says, "Just don't ever call me Mother."

(When it turns out Mother never was really married to Father, Jocelyn feels anything between her and Mister Boots is perfectly all right.)

So now there's another big tent set up not so far from our group of tents, but it doesn't have a yellow stripe; it has a big pink rose painted on it.

Pretty soon the show must go on.

My heart is broken. I have to leave the first and only friend I ever had. And now that our father is around more, I haven't had so many chances to be with her. I have to practice things and do my stretching exercises so as to get back in shape. Rosie is almost as free as I used to be back home. She doesn't have to do anything except help her mother at suppertime.

⌒⧓⌒

I sneak away to say good-bye to Rosie. As a going-away present I give her one of my twenty-dollar bills. She didn't know I was so rich. I tell her to keep it for something special and not to tell anybody.

She gives me a piece of dusty candy and a long blue ribbon. The ribbon is the only girl-type thing I ever had, except for knitting needles.

Rosie says some day this money might save her life, and that's true, it might.

On the way back I take the long way through the yellow grass to where a big batch of boulders fell down the hill and piled up. Rosie and I played house here. (I always had to be the husband.) I wanted to say good-bye to this place, too, but I come to a secret I shouldn't be seeing.

First I hear breathing. Snuffling kind of. I keep on walking around the stones, quietly, so as to sneak up and see what's happening—and then I wish I hadn't.

They're lying on an old army blanket so, for sure, they planned ahead. They're naked. (Jocelyn is almost as thin as Boots, but curvier.) I guess she finally convinced him.

At first I want to yell and stop them, but I'm not in the mood to scare people the way I usually like to do. And what they're about to do seems right. It *is* right—my sister's tawny, liony head next to the black-maned horsey one.

I shouldn't look.

I hear Boots say, "Sweet as grass. Sweet as apples."

I turn—from them and from the golden grass around them. I run back to Rosie. I don't tell her why. Rosie must think I'm going to get a whipping again. She says she'll hide me. Right now that's what I want the most. She has lots of good places and she takes me to her best one. She has to go help her mother, but I want to be alone anyway.

Before she leaves she says, "I don't blame you for being scared. The way your back looked. You had about the worst beating I ever saw on anybody."

In a funny way that makes me proud—as if I've passed some kind of test.

"Do you think that really was for your own good?"

I just shrug.

"Because whatever you think, it wasn't."

She hides me where there's an unused tent and an unused old wagon. She says, "There's mice and spiders out here, and rats and scorpions and rattlesnakes. . . ." She's trying to make me laugh, but why would I care if I'm a boy? So then she says, "Let's try to kiss our elbows again." We laughed a lot when we did that, but I'm not in the mood. Rosie has to go back to her mother anyway.

When I sit real still, pretty soon everything comes around, even a beautiful gopher snake. I'm so still he doesn't even care that I'm here. I think about love. I used to think it was wishy-washy. Then I think how our father always says magicians are special, and Lassiters are *especially* special, but I'm not sure about that anymore. Rosie is special.

I don't come back to our camping spot until dark. Mister Boots and my sister haven't changed that you can see. I'm the only one who knows they have.

They're all sitting around our campfire, which is just embers. Watching the fire is one of the nice things about this place. This is the last night for that. I'm not the only sad person. Tears make dark spots all over Jocelyn's tan blouse. She sits cross-legged, her knitting in her lap. Mister Boots has his arm around her on one side. I move close so I can lean against her on the other.

That lady is so far back from the fire, I almost forget she's here. She's still dressed up, even though she's just with us. She has bracelets practically up to her armpits, and she has that fur on her lap. She's stroking it as if it's alive. The bracelets catch the firelight sometimes, and so do the eyes of the fur. We're sitting on the ground, but she's on a chair she brought from her own tent. Dressed like that, you couldn't be on the ground. We're supposed to call her Aunt Tilly.

"All the ways to love," Boots says.

"Do tell," that lady says. The way she says it, I'll bet she can tell everything that happened today.

I think about that old poster and then I wonder, and then I ask, "Are you going to be in our act or what?"

She laughs a big, long laugh. The kind I didn't think

she ever would. (It doesn't fit with her fancy clothes.) She says, "I'm too fat to be onstage all dressed up in practically nothing, and too fat to get lifted up on nothing and too fat to even begin to get in the sword box."

"He's fatter."

"Don't be fooled. With me it's fat, but your father is strong as an ox."

"But you're all packed up to come along with us."

"Honey, it's a free ride."

So that's that then—good-bye to our camping in the country, to stream sounds, to trees-in-the-wind sounds, campfires, clumps of yellow grass. . . . But everybody's going off to bed just as if it's a completely ordinary, everyday night.

That lady takes up more space than any of us except our father. I think of all the things I could bring along if she wasn't here.

Mister Boots is the opposite. He says he never had so many things in his life before. His belongings take up one little box you can carry under your arm. He says he doesn't want one thing else except the scarf I'm knitting for him.

Riding down, that lady lets me wear her fur. I think it's because it's such a hot day she'd rather it be on me than on her. I don't care. I like wearing it no matter how hot.

I ask her what the fur's name is. At first she looks at me funny, and then like: Should she tell me? She squeezes her eyes shut and makes a face. (For a minute she reminds me of Rosie.)

She's sitting across from me in the car. I'm in the jump seat, and everybody is across from me. (Everybody except our father. He's with the wagon full of baggage.) It's sort of like being onstage, the three of them in front of me. This is the first time I've really looked at Aunt Tilly. Maybe she isn't what I thought she was.

"It used to be Wilhelmina," she says. "Funny, I haven't thought of that for a long time. You know boys don't wear furs."

"I don't care."

"You're a funny kid, you know that? How old are you really?"

At least she's not asking what sex I am.

"I'm . . ." But maybe I'm not supposed to tell my age even to her. "I can be any age you want."

She looks at me seriously for a minute and then crosses her eyes. You'd think she really was Rosie. You'd think she wasn't even ten years old yet.

Before, I thought she had a look about her as if, any minute, somebody was going to cheat her, even us, but on the ride down, she's more relaxed. She even sings. We'd join in except she's so good. We just listen. She sings "The Last Rose of Summer," and "My Wild Irish Rose," and "All Through the Night." She even brings tears to her own eyes and has to stop.

I say, "I'll bet you and our father used to sing together."

"We did. We sang onstage before we went into magic. That was a long time ago."

Then I ask Jocelyn why we can't live back at that camp all the time, like Rosie's family does.

She laughs as if it's a silly question. "Might as well go back home," she says, "where we have a nice little house all our own."

"No, I mean with other people around and campfires."

"Too many ants. . . . And, well, Rosie's very nice, but I don't trust those people. Like I told you before, they might be gypsies."

"They're not gypsies!"

Thinking of Rosie reminds me that I have the piece of dusty candy she gave me in my pocket. I suppose it's dustier than ever, but I put it in my mouth anyway. I try to do it in a way nobody can see, but that Aunt Tilly person notices and winks.

Our father's got three shows in a row lined up, in three schools. He's as nervous and blustery as usual, telling everybody what to do and to keep quiet and not to bother him with details.

Except that Tilly person talks about anything she feels like whenever she wants, and he lets her. Sometimes she tells him what to do, and he just goes ahead and does it.

It's Aunt Tilly who sews up the clown costume for

Mister Boots. I didn't think she'd sew. (She won't cook or do dishes. "Never again," she says. "I'd rather eat nothing but crackers and cheese than cook.")

She makes Boots a hobbyhorse, too, out of a mop, and with part of an old tire for a head. Boots gets a nose just like the one that clown at the camp wore all the time.

Nobody will ever get any acting out of Boots. So there's no such thing as rehearsing. He just is as he is. And how do we know he won't try to make another speech? I guess it won't matter; our father will make it part of his clowning like he did before.

One thing in all this bothers Mister Boots a lot. He keeps saying, "I ought to use whatever I have for a good purpose. I shouldn't waste it."

I always say, "First of all, what's good for one creature might be bad for another."

He always says, "True."

"And then how about worms?"

"Worms? What worms? Just because they're small. Why, without worms—"

I always say, "I know. You already told me about worms."

I have a whole new kind of costume, too. I'm not a pink pixie anymore. I'm a little version of our father, tails and all. We both wear a top hat, and we do duet kinds of things. I finally get a magic wand of my own, and I get to have a magic cane like his, and I get to do a cane dance duet with him where both our canes move by themselves. As we dance he keeps looking sideways at me with this grin. You're supposed to do that. And you're supposed to smile out over the people, too. My smile is like my voice: big. Onstage it's good to have a big mouth and black eyebrows and black hair like our father and I have. When we take our bows, our father holds my hand up and bows to me. Mostly I get a standing ovation. I bow even lower than our father taught me, my head right down on my knees. People laugh. Our father's too fat to bow that low.

When Aunt Tilly sees me onstage for the first time, she's impressed. Everybody always is. She feels about me the same as I do about our father. She said, "I don't care what age you are, you're good for any age there is," and, "Where did you get that voice?"

Before, I was thinking I'd borrow that fur and keep it hidden for a while with all the rest of my secret things, but I don't want to take anything from Aunt Tilly anymore. I'll just ask her—not if I can have it, but if I can sleep with it.

I don't want to ask her in front of everybody. I wait, and then I find the perfect place and time. We're in the writing room of the hotel. It's a fancy hotel, but I still like the tents better.

We're making lots of money, and we go all over the

place: Pasadena, Long Beach, Palm Springs . . . and all up and down the coast. I worry we won't be going back to that camping place again. I wonder if I'll ever see my one and only true friend.

I'm using the hotel stationery to write to Rosie, even though I don't know how to send the letter. Aunt Tilly said she'd see if it could be done. I have to make it simple because Rosie doesn't read very well even though she was homeschooled like I was.

Aunt Tilly is writing a letter, too, but she's staring out the window a lot. Anyway, she doesn't look bothered when I ask her, can I sleep with Wilhelmina.

"Are you still sleeping with things?"

"I never had anything to sleep with before. Anyway, I'm only seven."

"Whatever you say." And then, "You ever going to tell your old aunt Tilly anything that's true for once?"

"We live by lies."

"Who told you that? I suppose Mister Boots."

"No, that's what I say. Mister Boots would say the opposite, that we live by the truth."

"Is there something wrong with Mister Boots? He's so peculiar."

"It's everybody else who's peculiar."

But she just goes right on, her own way. "His voice is odd, too. Not like a foreigner, more like he isn't used to talking at all. Like he can't get his lips around the words. It's as if he's not right in the head. Sometimes he does sound wise, but it's . . . the wisdom of a child."

"People think he's dumb because they can't keep up with him. Besides, *I'm* a child."

She gets up and comes over to hug me. I let her. "A wise child," she says. Then, "Do you have any things? Toys, I mean? I haven't seen you with any."

First I think no, and then I remember my baseball and my mitt, but they're really our father's. I don't even like them, and I've never used them except that one time, so I say, "No."

"If you tell me how old you really are, you can sleep with Wilhelmina."

I finally get a chance to not be seven. "I'm the perfect age," I say.

"I know what that is. I'll bet you're ten."

At the hotel, I finally get to hear Aunt Tilly and our father sing duets. I was in bed, but then I hear singing and I know it's them. I get dressed (those knickers and my sweater) and put Wilhelmina around my neck, but I go down only as far as the landing just in case they see me and make me go back upstairs. Aunt Tilly is playing the piano. She can do most everything. They sing "Oh Promise Me," and "The Last Rose of Summer," and "Love's Old Sweet Song," and "Old

Black Joe." I have to wipe my tears on Wilhelmina.

The hotel guests clap a lot. The bellboys, too. I hope everybody knows that that's my father and my . . . not my aunt, stepmother really. I can't believe how, at first, I didn't like Aunt Tilly.

Pretty soon the time comes for Boots to do his act. I'm the one to lead him out onstage again. I help him into his costume. He wouldn't do that either if not for me. The costume hangs on him. I say, "Hello, Droopy." I want to make him laugh, but he just droops more than ever.

Aunt Tilly is right; his face is odd. I see that even more as I put red spots on his cheeks and then lipstick on him. I stick on the nose ball. "Are you sad?"

"As a human being in a world of human beings? Never sad."

I don't want him thinking too much about going out onstage so I say, "Mister Boots, there's a secret, and you're not going to believe it."

This will make him sit up and take notice. Maybe even make him change to Moonlight Blue right here and now.

The thing is, everybody is forgetting what I am, what with these boy clothes all the time and the talk about, "My son this and my son that." Everybody! Even Jocelyn. I have a hard time keeping track of myself myself. I want to tell somebody.

But Boots says, "You don't have to tell me. Sometimes it's better not to know, but I will believe what you want me to."

"I want you to hear it."

He says, "What you tell will not be wasted."

"Oh, Mister Boots . . . You tell me something instead."

"What I have to say is, I want to live a life of service to all beings."

"You're too nice, horse or man. Sometimes you have to try not to be."

"You should help me with my message."

"I will, but later. Now we have to do this. We'll trot out pretending to be horses. I'll pretend it, too. Your whinny? Remember that? It's a good one. We'll whinny together and lope in circles."

"No!"

"You told me once yourself there are a hundred different ways of seeing the exact same thing."

"I can't this minute see more than two ways."

"Oh, Boots! All right, you hang on to the lead rope and I'll lope in."

Instead of my main secret I tell him a different one. I tell him, "One of these days—pretty soon now—I'm going to let the doves go."

I thought he'd like that, but he's not sure they'll be able to survive on their own.

Our father has a half dozen old pots and pans piled up in the wings all ready for Mister Boots, just in case he has to do the same as last time. I get myself ready, too—for anything.

So Mister Boots walks out onstage in front of me with a long, long, long lead rope. People even think that's funny. Boots is halfway across the stage before I finally jig in, wearing my dress suit and a halter. I whinny my whinny. I jump around (shy, that is) with sudden twists to the side. I don't have to practice any of it. There's nothing horse-ish I haven't done already.

People laugh like anything. It doesn't matter now what Boots does. I'm being a pretty good horse myself. I'm even funnier, dressed in my dress suit, cavorting like a crazy person, my tails flying; and Boots is on his hobbyhorse looking at me, so sad and serious . . . that's funny, too. Our father didn't want us to do it like this, but if it works, he won't mind.

If Boots was planning on doing his speechifying about letting every single creature go free, he gets it knocked right out of him. He steps to the side as if to escape all my jumping around, but with that droopy clown suit—the legs hanging over his big phony shoes—he falls flat on his back. Hard. And right after . . .

He changed. . . . I'm pretty sure he did. Maybe out of fear and pain. He did, but for such a tiny moment, and like he didn't mean to. I'm not sure it really happened. I just saw the flash of a white horse. Rearing. And then there was Boots, lying there, looking as surprised as I was.

Everybody is looking at me, but I hear a few people gasp. I look back at our father, in the wings. He's wiping the sweat off his face with a big towel. He didn't see either, but he suspects.

I help Boots off the stage. Slowly. He's dazed and hurt some. I yell, "Come on, White Lightning."

I keep telling Aunt Tilly I wish she'd get sawed in half like she used to do. She always says, "Fat-lady-gets-sawed-in-half-no-thank-you." So I have to keep on doing it, even though I always get itchy in there. (I change to the pixie costume for that and the sword box.)

Things go along pretty well, though twice our father gets his grocery-store whip out again. Just for on my legs. I wonder who he used it on when he wasn't around us. For sure not Aunt Tilly. She's one of those people you don't mess with.

Aunt Tilly always has her own room, though she sometimes sleeps with our father. "Rich or poor," she says, "I get to have my own room." What Aunt Tilly wants, she always gets.

chapter ten

I'm getting known all over. I can't walk down the street without that somebody knows me. The problem is, I want to go off, for once in my life, wearing a dress. Just to see what it's like, but will everybody recognize me? My short hair is a big clue, but I hope, if I'm wearing a dress, they'll think: This can't be him—the one and only famous Robert Lassiter, Jr.

The reason I'm thinking about a dress right now is, there's a girl at our hotel and she's pretty much my size. I don't want to get to know her, because she's not like Rosie, and I promised Rosie she would be my best friend for life. This girl's name is Madelaine-Ellen and everybody calls her the *whole* thing. I don't know if I could stand doing that. She goes to church with her parents and her brother, so I know exactly when and where to get a dress. I'll pick a plain one so I won't be too noticeable.

I'll have to be bold, but magic is being bold all the time.

But when it comes right down to it, I don't pick a plain dress, I pick one I like. It looks as if it ought to be mine in the first place. It's brown with little black outlines of flowers all over it, and little yellow dots in the center of each flower. It has a white, boy-type collar, so it's not prissy.

I bring it back to my room to try it on.

I'm thinner than that girl, so the dress doesn't look very good. I say, "Hello, Droopy," to myself. I guess whatever dress I borrow, I'll look like a clown anyway. My short hair adds to the clown look. Girls don't have hair like this unless they just had head lice.

I watch myself in the mirror and practice how to be a girl. It feels funny. Airy. Maybe I'm supposed to have a slip. I practice looking delicate. Except Rosie wasn't like that. She was even tougher than me. Maybe as tough as Aunt Tilly. The more I think about it, the more I don't know how I should behave.

The dress has pockets. I'll bring along forty dollars and flash paper and the little magic lighter. I won't take the pistol. The pockets aren't big enough.

I don't want anybody around the hotel to see me, so, although I love the elevator and the elevator man, I take the stairs. There's nobody. Who would be there when you could ride in the elevator instead?

I run across the lobby as fast as I can, out the hotel door, and down the street. I don't look to see who's watching, I just go and keep on going. Then I slow down and walk— still pretty fast though. Nobody pays attention. Is this all there is to it?

There's a nice big park with swings and slides and teeter-totters. I've seen it as we passed by on the way to someplace else, but I never got to go there. I wasn't heading for it now, but here it is. Since it's Sunday morning there's nobody around. I sit on the bottom of a teeter-totter and wish Rosie were here to get on the other end. I think how my skirt goes up and my underwear shows, which is boy's underwear.

Then I put my skirt under me and slide the slides, all of them, even the baby one, and then I swing. (It's the opposite of the dressy tails of my costume. Those you have to *not* sit on. If I don't put the skirt under me the seat is scratchy. That's another girl thing you have to find out.)

It's a wonder I even know how to swing, but I catch on fast. I feel scared and embarrassed even though there's nobody here, except I feel good, too, but then I start to feel sad. It isn't that I want to wear dresses so much, I don't; it's more that I can never be the truth about myself. And when I think how I've hardly ever been in a playground and how Rosie is my only friend and I had to say good-bye to her forever.

All of a sudden I have to swing really hard and high. I go so high the ropes of the swing get loose at the top of the arc.

I wonder if you could go all the way around. I wouldn't like to do that, but I keep on, swinging hard.

Somebody has been watching me all this time, and I didn't even know it—all this time that I've been looking at my boy's underwear and pulling down my skirt.

I don't see him till he gets up and starts toward me. I'm still swinging to beat the band, and I keep on. He'd better not come too close or I'll kick him in the jaw. "Right on the button." That's what our father says.

Except he does come close. He's angry already, and I haven't said a single word. It's as if he already knows everything about me and doesn't like any of it.

I can smell him, even though I'm swishing back and forth making my own breeze.

He says, "If you were good, you'd be in church."

I keep swinging hard. "So would you. Besides . . ." (More lies. Why not?) "My mother and my father and my two big brothers . . . *They're* there. That counts."

"If you don't go to church, you'll think there isn't any hellfire. You'll go bad."

"What about you then?"

That's when he grabs me. It stops the swing so fast I nearly fall off. My skirt is up around my waist. He pulls me all the way off and pulls my skirt even higher.

"You can't fool me. You're really a boy."

I try to get away. He hangs on and laughs. "Boys like you go straight to hell. You can struggle all you want, it's hellfire top to bottom. All the way down."

Then he grabs me right *there* and says, "Well, well, well," surprised, and pushes me flat on my back, pulls my underpants to my knees, and takes a long look. (How long does it take for him to see that I'm a girl?) And then he takes a feel.

He's so smelly I can hardly stand it. But I can't stand *any* of it. Not for a single minute more.

"I have money."

At least that makes him feel for my pockets instead of me. He pulls out my two twenties and then my flash paper, which looks to him like a little nothing tablet. He takes the money and throws the paper down beside us.

"A lot of money for a little whore like you. You'll burn in hellfire for what you do."

He holds me down with his knee across my stomach and tries to put the money in his pocket, but that pocket has a hole in it so he has to find another. He keeps mumbling about how I'll burn in hellfire. Hellfire is his favorite word.

He can't find a pocket without holes. He even keeps trying the same pockets. He's got me pinned, but he's not watching. I get out the tiny magic lighter that fits on the tips of my fingers.

I never did light a whole tablet before, but I always wanted to.

It makes a big, big flash. It burns my face and I'll bet his, too. More so, because I threw it right at him.

He gives a screech and yells, "Hellfire!"

It's as if I had looked straight into the sun. By the time I can see again, he's way, way, way across at the far side of the park and still going, stumbling like he's blinded even more than I am.

I pull my underpants up and dust myself off. I'm a mess. I'm crying, but everybody would cry after this sort of thing, even boys.

I run all the way back. All the way up the stairs. I just want to be by myself and wash off the smell from that man.

And there's Aunt Tilly—coming out her door just as I'm going into mine. I try to escape and shut my door on her, but she grabs it and comes right in. I'm still running—to the far corner of the room and then it's as if I'm running still but there's no place to go. She grabs me and holds me tight. She's a strong lady, and I don't really want to get away.

Pretty soon she pulls back to look at me. At the dress. It's torn. It's dirty. I'm dirty. I know I smell bad, too, just like that man.

I don't say a word. I couldn't if I wanted to. First I look down because I don't want to look at her face, and then I do look, and after I'm looking into her eyes, I stay like that. I don't even dare move my eyeballs. Aunt Tilly looks like she doesn't dare either. She's perfectly still, but I can see her thoughts are going round and round inside her.

She says, "My poor . . . Oh, my poor . . ." It's as if she just this minute realized she doesn't know my name, which she doesn't.

She's wearing Wilhelmina. She takes her off and wraps her around me.

"For you. For forever."

Suddenly I realize my fingers are burned and my face feels sunburned and my feet hurt from running in my shoes that are too big. . . .

We go down on the floor then, both of us, Aunt Tilly as big as she is. She leans her back against the bed and holds my head to her big . . . first I'm thinking what Rosie called them: "lung warts" and "knockers." She's squashy all over. I always was thinking before how she should be slim like Mother was, but I don't think that anymore.

I try to tell her things, but I can't, and she says, "Not now. Just cry. Poor little girl."

I do cry. And, even though I'm ten, it doesn't matter being called little.

Aunt Tilly gives me a bath, and I'm in it utterly naked. The real me. She washes me *everywhere*. She bandages my burned fingers. (She puts unsalted butter on them and on my face.) She dresses me in my boy pajamas and helps me into bed.

And all the time she keeps shaking her head as if everything is, no, no, no, no, no. Then she brings hot milk with vanilla and nutmeg, and she sits next to me while I doze. Every time I move or open my eyes a little bit, she pats my hand.

She says she'll wash and repair the dress but she'll not give it back, so we're in this together now. Then Aunt Tilly says, "Who else knows about you?" and I say, "Just my sister."

"So we'll keep it that way for now."

She sits with me until we hear our father calling her. He's knocking on her door and yelling, "Dear!" His stage voice as always.

I'm thinking he wouldn't dare walk right into her room. He doesn't dare anything against Aunt Tilly, and now she's on my side.

Aunt Tilly says, "There's my hippopotamus of a lover." She pats me again. "Are you going to be all right?"

"Now I am."

She kisses me, a big loud smack, and then she kisses Wilhelmina just the same way. "I'll check on you when I come up to bed."

Things change. Not only do I get a rest because of my burned fingers, but suddenly I get to have toys, and not just boy things—kind of half and half. I get to have a little green felt elephant. I get to have a great big Puss in Boots. I get to wear Wilhelmina all day long. I get to have licorice sticks. Our father doesn't like it, but he has nothing to say about it.

When Aunt Tilly puts her foot down, it stays put down.

Sometimes it seems our father really is in love with Aunt Tilly and she really is in love with him.

I don't understand love at all.

Me being a boy is the most important thing there is in his life. Aunt Tilly said he won't let go of an idea he needs as much as this one: his son and heir, to carry on the name and the profession. Aunt Tilly said that's what my mother was for. When Aunt Tilly told him she wasn't about to have a child for him, let alone keep on having them until there was a son or two, he went off to find somebody who would.

She said, "If he hadn't, you and Jocelyn wouldn't exist, so *two* good things came of it."

And then she warns me. "If he finds out! Having a son is what his whole life is about, though he doesn't like children." Then she says, "Any more than I do," and kisses me—again one of those loud comedy kisses, but I can tell those are real.

"But, Aunt Tilly, he didn't ever come around back home. I didn't even know him. Once he tried to teach me things for the show, just once, but then . . . Aunt Tilly, you know how he twists people's arms up behind them? I think he broke my arm. And then he left for years and years."

"I suppose that scared him off for a while. He's not as sure of himself as he seems."

chapter eleven

Then the Depression hits, and it doesn't take long for us to get poor along with everybody else, because nobody can afford to go to shows like ours. We lower the price to the absolute lowest we can, to just a nickel. But I don't care how poor we get, I still have almost all my secret money.

We still perform, but in smaller places and not so often. Sometimes in parks, except we have to be careful nobody gets behind us and finds out things. There's some tricks we don't do because of that. Sometimes our father and I go off alone and perform on street corners. I pass my top hat. We've come down that far. I guess it's down—our father says it is—but I like it.

We go to that very same park and there's that very same man. I see he knows me even though I'm in my dress suit, top hat, and everything. We're on the back of a rented truck. Everybody watching has to stand up or sit on the grass. This man stands right in the middle and right in front of everybody. I'm scared. I don't stick to our plans. Before we even get started, I throw fire, three quick batches right toward him. I'm wasting flash paper. It costs a lot.

This time the fire doesn't scare the man. I'm not close enough to blind him like before. He ducks but then comes right up, grabs my leg, and pulls me off the truck. "You little bitch. Whores like you end up in hellfire. I say hellfire!" And he starts to shake me really hard.

This man is tall and our father isn't, but, like Aunt Tilly said, our father's pretty much all muscle. I always think fat, but she's right, it's not. He's one of those people all chest and shoulders and gorilla arms. He jumps off the truck, grabs that tall man, and tosses him away as if he was as small I am. The man picks himself up and leaves, but he keeps on yelling back at us. "You're nothin' but a girl. She's a girl, everybody. You're wasting your money. She's not worth shit. She's not even worth hellfire."

Our father hears it, but it washes right off him. I guess it washes off everybody, or, girl or boy, they don't care. Our father gives me a hug. (That's the first time for that. I thought he didn't believe in hugs for boys.) Then he lifts me up to the truck.

It's lucky I don't have my pistol; I'm so mad I would have shot that bum.

Then we really do run out of money. Aunt Tilly doesn't have her bracelets halfway up her arms anymore. (Some of those were real gold.) Her fuzzy red hair has whitish roots that aren't curly. My sister begins to knit the way she used to. I help some, but I'm slow and I'm still not good at much more than scarves, except Mister Boots likes his, just the way it is. Mine is the first and only scarf he ever had.

Boots has always worked on our packing and loading and setting up, but now he works for other people, too. He does all kinds of things, but what he likes best is to work with animals. He shovels out stables and paddocks. He loves to curry and hose down horses. He loves the smell of the bales of hay. Lots of times I go with him and help. I want to, because I worry that he'll let the horses go or get himself in trouble some other way. I work hard when I'm with him, but they don't pay me except a nickel now and then. They always say I'm too little to do a good job. Mister Boots doesn't think that. He'd give me half what he earns, but I tell him to give it to Jocelyn for more oatmeal and beans.

When he's working at the racetrack and watches the horses practice, I've seen him look as if he's going to change to Moonlight Blue right then and there in order to race with them. He gets covered with sweat just from watching. I'm surprised he doesn't run out on the track even as a mere man. When I see Boots like that, I know why people always say, "Hold your horses." I say it. I take a tight hold on his arm. "Hold your horses, Mister Boots."

There's another reason I like to go off to help Boots. Our father is getting mad at everything. He's not a drinker, but you'd think he was, the way he rages around and slaps his hand against doorways and tables even when everything seems perfectly fine to me. Aunt Tilly says she might be the only person who can take care of us.

She *could* leave. She can take care of herself. She said, "I've earned my living from the age of twelve, mostly by getting myself sawed in half or raised up in the air. And I did all those same important things *you* do while people have their eyes on Robert. Can you imagine? Buxom at twelve? Nobody guessed how young I was. Can you imagine me getting in that box and getting myself sawed in half again *now*? Imagine the box he'd need!" And then she throws back her head and laughs her big laugh.

At last we go back to the tent place. We go up the way we did before, a motorcar for us and a wagon for our tents and boxes of magic stuff. All the way there I'm so happy I can't sit still.

(I think Houdie got sold a long time ago, but our father won't say. He gets angry even if I just look like I'm going to ask about him, but I think it was Houdie money that paid for us to come up here in a car.)

Because of the Depression, the tent place is different from before. It's full up, but not with many circus people anymore. We sneak in and share a spot with another family. We pay them two bits a week for taking up half their space. Lots of people are doing that.

I look all over, but Rosie isn't there, and the place where

Rosie hid me—with the old tent and the broken-down cart beside it—is completely changed. The bushes are cut down to make more room, and there's two families crowded in there.

Did Rosie's family get too poor for even two bits' worth of space? They never took up much room. They could squeeze in with us. I'd pay.

A few days later, after I've given up, I do find Rosie—down the road a piece. I find her by mistake. Our father and I are looking for a good and cheap space to give one of our shows, like a barn where we can charge admission, not a park where I have to pass the hat. Our father likes to take me any place that involves exercise and fresh air. He says, "A healthy mind in a healthy body." As if he hasn't told me that dozens of times already.

He always walks me out as fast as he can go. Same reason. Every single time I'm with him I have to trot to keep up. So here I am, trotting along, and I see Rosie's tent, small and raggedy, and no sign of a car or a horse or a wagon. There's a piece of an old tarp propped sideways against sagebrush for a little bit of shade. It's just behind an irrigation ditch that doesn't have any water in it. There's a runty little half-dead tree making a few more sticks of shade. Rosie is under it, washing dishes in a pail and basin. I wonder where she gets water?

Since I'm with our father, I don't let on to Rosie that I see her. I wiggle my fingers behind my back. Last thing, I try to kiss my elbow. When I turn around, I see she's laughing so hard her head is practically in the dishpan.

Our father and I find a good barn-dance barn not far from where Rosie is camped. I'm happy because she'll get to see me. Before we perform I'm going to tell her I'm a girl, so she'll know girls can do it just as well as anybody.

That evening I sneak out, all the way back. It's cool, a good chance to wear Wilhelmina, and anyway I want to show her off. The minute we see each other we start to giggle. We don't hug or touch or say anything. We just stand there and shrug our shoulders. Finally we sit down on the ditch bank a little ways from her tent. We still don't say anything, as if suddenly we don't know each other anymore, even though it hasn't been that long.

But I want to find out, why are they way down here and not up in the tent place?

She says her father ran off. (I tell her that always happens.) Now there's just her and her mother, and she has to do all the work because her mother has this weakness. Rosie says it's hard getting food and hard carrying water way out here, and they haven't enough money to stay with the tents. In fact they haven't any money at all. (The twenty dollars I gave her got used up a long time ago.) Mostly she doesn't know what to do. She thinks her mother should see a doctor, but she doesn't know how to get her to one. When her father went off, he took the flivver.

When she starts to tell me, she gets shaky. I know how scary it is when there's something wrong with your mother, and she hasn't even got a big sister to help her.

Rosie isn't like she used to be. She's too worried and she's working too hard. We won't have time to play.

I give her forty dollars, which I brought along specially. (My pile of money is still just as big as ever.)

Rosie looks at me funny.

"I didn't steal it. Honest. And I have more if you need it. You can use it to get your mother to the doctor."

I feel so sorry for her I almost give her Wilhelmina, but she'd probably sell her, and I don't ever want Wilhelmina sold.

It's pretty late when I walk back from Rosie's. The almost-full moon is coming up. I stay away from the road even if it means walking through all kinds of scratchy things. (It's good I'm wearing knickers.) Part of the time I walk in the empty ditch where it's not so bushy. When cars come by, I step away from their lights. Ever since that man in the park, I'm careful.

Whenever there's moonlight like this, I think about how Moonlight Blue looked the first time I saw him as a horse.

What if he came galloping by right now, *thumpety, thumpety, thump*ing up to me? I haven't ridden a horse for a long time, and that's one of my most favorite things.

When I get back, I see Boots and Jocelyn by the fire. I sit across from them. Boots lifts her hand to his lips and kisses the palm. How did a horse learn a thing like that?

A couple of days go by and I haven't gone back to see Rosie. I worry about her, but it's a long walk and I haven't much time. I have to keep in practice. But all of a sudden here's Rosie, in the middle of the night, in my tent! In my bed! First I try to get in bed and then I give a yell because I think it's got to be that dirty old bum from the park. Thank goodness Jocelyn doesn't sleep with me anymore. She and Boots have a pup tent of their own.

I say, "Shhhhh." I look outside to see if anybody heard. Jocelyn calls, "Are you all right?" I say, "Just a spider." Then I say, "One of those giant barn spiders. I'm bringing it out to you." And then I laugh a Halloween kind of laugh. I do all that because I don't usually yell for spiders since that's a girl thing. I didn't even do that back before our father came when I knew, better than I know now, that I'm a girl.

We can't talk; Mister Boots and my sister and Aunt Tilly are too nearby. Rosie does tell me that they took her mother to the hospital and that she doesn't want to be alone down there by the ditch.

I tell her she can stay here forever if she needs to.

We cuddle up. There's not much room, so there's no way not to. She cries for a while. I can tell, though she doesn't make a single sound. Then I think she's asleep, but all of a sudden I feel her hand on me and she says, "You're a girl." I say, "I know." And then I say, "Don't tell," and she says, "Of course not." She says, "Besides, I knew it all the time."

In the morning I sneak her biscuits with lots of apple butter just the way I like them. She says she shouldn't have so much, it's expensive, but I say I want her to. Then I show her where I keep the money and the pistol.

I tell her I'll only shoot bad people. And now that she knows where it is, she can do that, too, if she needs to.

(I usually keep it in sort of the same place it was when Mother hid it. I stick it up under my cot with adhesive tape. I tell her that has to be a good spot since I'm the only one who found it in the first place. But I have to be sure to take it down when the cot's going to be folded up.

Then I have to leave to go practice with our father.

The next day I worry about Rosie not having things to do, stuck there in a tent that's only a little bit bigger than a pup tent, but she just sleeps, as if she's catching up for a long time of worry. Later a person drives into our tent city looking for her. He says her mother's dying and she should come. Jocelyn says Rosie's not around here that she knows of, but I say I know where she is and I'll go get her.

For a day and a half I don't have to worry about us getting found out, but then she comes back, because her mother died. This time she hitchhiked back. It took her most of the day. She didn't know where else to go. I tell her, "You did right. I have enough of everything for two."

The minute she gets here she goes out by herself for a while, out where those rocks are—where we used to play and where I saw Mister Boots and Jocelyn except I left before it happened. When she comes back, she just wants to sleep again. She says she isn't hungry, though you'd think she would be after a couple of days like these last two. I bring her cookies anyway, for later. I put them in a can with a tight lid because of mice.

I guess Rosie won't be able to appreciate seeing me perform. I don't think she even cares if she comes or just lies here in the tent staring into space. It's sure not hard to keep her a secret.

But I want her to see me. I tell her I'll feel bad if she doesn't come and doesn't like me. She says she isn't in the mood for liking things even if it's me. I say, "There'll always be plenty of other times for staring into space, and I think it's not good for you to stay in here all the time."

Our father and I put up posters that say, SPECIAL HOLIDAY RATES, and ONE-TIME PERFORMANCE. LASSITER THE GREAT AND SON, PRIZES AND FREE RABBITS.

I ask our father for a free ticket. Just one. In all this time, I never have asked, not even once. And we're only charging a nickel. (The farmer who owns the barn is going to get half.) Jocelyn hears me, and when our father says, "What do you want a ticket for?" she stops knitting and says, "One ticket, for heaven's sake! He doesn't have to tell you everything."

"Since when?"

"Since all the time."

She puts her knitting down and stands up. I love that she's as tall as our father, and I love her when she stands up and looks like this.

She says, "I'm tired of all this. I've a good mind to just take Bobby and . . . Mister Blue . . . and go back home for some peace and quiet. Bobby has rights."

"Control yourself, for heaven's sake."

"Control!"

She turns her back, picks up her knitting, and goes out. But I get a ticket.

Later I asked Aunt Tilly, "How come, for a person who says he never loses his temper, he's the worst of anybody? And why all the time mad at me?"

She says it's because I'm so special to him. "He wants to live his life over again through you. You're of no use to him as a girl. When . . ." (She says, "When.") "When he finds out . . . ! You know he doesn't know his own strength. You come to me. Right off, you hear? You come straight to me."

I have a dream about it. In my dream our father is like that bull at the rodeo we saw. We saw this bull bang into fences and chase people. He knocked a man down and trampled all over him. So I dream a bull like that but black and white, as if in a dress suit. It pulls down all our tents and tramples everything, and then it throws Wilhelmina in the fire. Wilhelmina cries *baa, baa,* like a little lamb. In the dream I try to rescue her. There's this terrible bellowing all through the dream. I wake myself up making bellowing sounds myself, as if I'm the crazy angry bull.

Rosie wakes me to stop my nightmare, but Jocelyn is already rushing in like she always does when I have a bad dream. She's brought her flashlight, and first thing she shines it right on Rosie. I can't see her face with the light in my eyes. I can't tell what she's thinking. I say, "But her mother died." Then Jocelyn kneels beside us and first hugs Rosie and then me. She sits for a while smoothing our hair back from our foreheads and stroking our cheeks, alternating me and Rosie. She keeps saying, "Everything's all right," even to Rosie.

We load up and go to have our barn show. We put up our little stage and our wings and our backdrop and our lights. I dress in my dress suit and get our tricks ready. Boots is ready, looking droopy in his clown suit with his halter dangling.

I peek out from the wings. The barn is getting full. Everybody from the camp who can afford a nickel is there; all the farmers come, too. Everybody is dressed in their best. We were smart because our father and the farmer are having a barn dance afterward. The farmer's wife looks happy. She and Jocelyn are at the door taking in money and tickets. Rosie came down by herself so our father wouldn't know about her staying with us. She's already here in a good front seat—on a pillow on the ground. I told her to bring our pillow.

As usual I'm a big hit even the minute I come onstage. Our father always does a few things first and then I come on and everybody yells. Mostly sport-type things like, "Go, Bobby!" And right away I don't mind having to be seven anymore.

Rosie thinks it's all real. She's like I used to be. When I'm in the sword box getting swords stuck into it, I hear Rosie yell not to do it. That's when she starts to cry. After that she cries all through. I suppose it's really her mother she's thinking of. Jocelyn goes and sits beside her and holds her hand. And then I see they're both crying.

Then comes the part where Boots and I come in at a slow lope, his floppy shoes flap, flapping. Everybody laughs, except Rosie keeps on crying.

And then, all of a sudden, there's this gasping sound— everybody gasping at the same time. I look around to see what's wrong; is the barn burning down? Then I know it's got to be Moonlight Blue! I don't know why he does it. He does it and then just stays in one spot as if he *is* a mirror trick and doesn't dare move out of the mirror's range. But then he stamps and thumps on our stage floor with his unshod hoofs. It makes a nice racket. His ears are pricked up as if everything is fine. He looks good, shiny white in the lights and bigger, like our father always seems. Everybody oohs and aahs, and I yell, "Yes!" I can't help it. This is even better than sunsets and even better than Aunt Tilly's songs.

Our father doesn't get to see the change. He always takes the moment we're onstage alone to wipe his hands and face and change what he has in his coattails. I see him come and look, but it's too late. Boots is back. First I think he did it for me, and then I think, No, it's special for Rosie.

After it's over, the barn dance and all, we sit around the fire back at our camping spot like we do. It's late, but we're still too excited even to think of going to bed. I ask Mister Boots why did he, all of a sudden, do it?

Rosie is with us. She has a midnight snack with us right out in front of everybody. Nobody says a word about her being here. If our father was here, he would have for sure, but he went off to town wearing his turban. When he's away like this, I always know that's where he is, not drinking much, but singing and doing tricks and getting admired and talking about me.

It's cool. I guess fall is coming. Aunt Tilly has on a black shawl that's so lacy I don't see how there can be any warmth to it. Boots is wearing his red sweater. I'm letting Rosie wear Wilhelmina, but I tell her I can't—I just *can't*—give her to her. She doesn't mind, long as she can borrow it now and then.

Mister Boots says, "Money isn't everything." Is that supposed to be my answer?

"That's what I think, too," says my sister.

I don't say it, but I'm thinking: Then why did we all run around like crazy people looking for the knitting money?

"But, Mister Boots, tonight . . . ? Why did you do it, all of a sudden, tonight?"

"I saw Rosie—I saw you, Rosie and you were crying, and I thought how I said before that everybody should think and I thought I should think, too, and what I thought was: Do ideas come from words? Or do ideas come from things? Or do they come from actions? It was an action and an idea and a thing."

I suppose that's an explanation.

Aunt Tilly doesn't say a word. What I like about her is she knows when to keep quiet.

chapter twelve

After this barn performance, we don't have any more shows lined up. Our father tries. Sometimes he's gone for days, but he always comes back with nothing, or nothing worth taking all of us to. He does a little show now and then by himself. I guess that's why we're not starving. And then there's the knitting. That still sells a little.

It's hard to believe, but he's getting even angrier than he already was. The good thing about it is, he gets quiet this time. He hardly seems to be with us when he's with us. Aunt Tilly says it's never been this bad. She says he's really scared.

Another good thing is, he doesn't care anymore if I stand up straight or not, or if I get my exercise and my sunshine every day, and breathe deeply of this country air. He used to tell me, "Practice, practice, practice," and then, "Practice doesn't make perfect, practice makes permanent; only perfect practice makes perfect." I couldn't count the times he's said that, but he doesn't say it anymore.

Now he just sits and stares, or wanders about in his

purple turban smoking cigars. (We have to cut back on everything, so how come he gets to have his cigars? I'll bet Aunt Tilly could have her hair back red and curly if she had his cigar money. I'd give her some of my money, but that would bring up too many questions.)

Our father doesn't seem to notice anything about Rosie. You'd think he would, considering she's another mouth to feed.

There's a batch of bums always hanging around. I don't know why they pick other poor people to beg from. But then everybody's poor now. People do share things a lot, but these bums steal from the farmers—corn and grapes—and try to sell them to us, so the farmers are against us, too. The problem is, they want the camp removed and all of us thrown out. We're a blot on the whole neighborhood.

They're going to make us leave, and then they're going to burn the place to get rid of the fleas. All of a sudden we have one week to get out of here before they kick us out. Rosie and I want to go to town, so I guess we have to go right now.

These days everybody hitchhikes, but Jocelyn says, for me, it's strictly forbidden, even though she used to have to do it all the time. I'm the only, only one who's not allowed to.

I want to buy a couple of dresses for Rosie. Everything she owns is falling apart. And I want to get us nice shoes.

All I have are boy's ones, and they're *still* too big. I'll get
Rosie anything she wants, and we'll have maple walnut
sundaes. Maybe even two or three.

But in town everybody looks at us funny. They think it's
odd that kids our age should have money. (Neither of us
look as old as we really are.) We have to change our plans.
I tell Rosie, "Let's buy watches. We can say they're gifts for
our mothers and our dads gave us the money for them." All
I do is make her cry because her mother would have wanted a watch. And I make myself feel bad for the same reasons, even though my mother had one. But I can't let
myself cry, so then I say, real quick, "Let's get some banjos."
I want to make her laugh, but it doesn't work, so to cheer
ourselves up we go for ice-cream sundaes right away. That'll
be an early lunch. Later we'll do it again for another lunch.

Then we go to the secondhand store. There, people
don't look at us so suspiciously.

I buy Rosie two dresses for ten cents each. For a nickel
I get her a lady's purse that's hardly worn out at all. For
myself I get a rusty old harmonica that only cost two pen-
nies. I'd better not let our father see it. He'll say it's full of
germs.

On the way back, that same farmer from where we gave our
show recognizes me and picks us up in his rattly truck. He
keeps talking about how wonderful our father is. How

proud I must be, of him and of myself, too. And if our father wants a job helping out on the farm, he'll put us up. Not much pay, but we'd have a place to stay. I say I don't think our father knows anything about farming. (The truth is our father would rather starve than be anything but a magician—or maybe a singer.)

The farmer doesn't take us all the way to the camp. We have to walk the last three or so miles. He says he's tired, but I'll bet we're tireder than he is. How come he lets two children who he thinks are only seven years old go off by themselves like this? And it'll be dark by the time we get back.

But I don't mind. We watch our long shadows. Our shadow heads go all the way to the edge of the first hills until the sun goes behind the mountains on the opposite side.

Even though it's late, we hear a racket as we get close to the camp, which is odd because it's a family kind of place. Usually by this time it's nice and quiet: soft talk around the fires, maybe a little music going on here and there, but the closer we get, the more it sounds like a riot. Then we see tents getting taken down and hear babies crying as if they all got wet and hungry at the same time, and people are running back and forth and there's soldiers and police and they have their pistols and rifles out. It's like we're all criminals.

We were supposed to have three days more, but they've come early. I hear people say they did that on purpose, came at night, too, so we wouldn't be ready.

Then I see people starting to get quiet and crowding over toward our place, and I see our father standing up on the back of somebody's truck telling jokes and doing tricks. His voice is sounding out over all the people's heads like it always does. People are calming down and laughing and bunching up around him. The whole spirit is changing. Camp people and soldiers stand next to one another and laugh together. All over again I'm thinking: *My* father. *Mine!* He's making everybody laugh and making everybody get along with one another.

He brings out the last of our rabbits (there're only four left), and every time he makes one appear out of his top hat he gives it to a soldier or a policeman. And then our father sees me and waves me over and says, "Lassiter and Son. *And* Son!" like he's as proud of me, right this minute, as I am of him. Then he has me come up on the bed of the truck and do tricks, too. He stands to the side and claps for me. "Let's give the boy a big hand," and they do. I thought I was all worn out and couldn't wait to get to bed, but I'm not tired now.

Before we've hardly finished the act, the army wants us to put on a show for them, and if we're gone we can't do it. So there's a lot of talk and then our father and the head of the camp and the sheriff go away, and pretty soon they come back and we not only get our three days, but a whole week more on top of that, all because of our father.

But people don't trust the police. A lot of them move out right away. They were already half packed up, anyway. Instead of being overfull, all of a sudden the camp is half empty. It's nice this way.

We have to get ready for the big army show, so I have to keep in practice, but I find some time to be with Rosie. We go back to the boulders where we used to play. The bums are gone, chased out I guess, and it's a mess, old rusty cans and pans and bottles and pieces of dirty tarp, but all the better for playing house.

We change around. Sometimes Rosie is the husband, and I'm the wife. I say, All right, I'll be a wife, but no spankings. She says she wouldn't do that to me anyway, even if I did a very bad thing.

Rosie wears her new dresses all the time, even out there to play in the dirt. Sometimes she changes so as to wear both in one day. She carries her purse everywhere, too. It's already full of useful things—safety pins and rubber bands and money that I gave her in case of emergency. But I don't play my rusty harmonica much. The rust hurts my lips. Actually I'm a little worried about germs on it myself.

At the army camp we do our whole big show, and our father and I do doves together and do our cane duet, and our father looks at me like I'm the best thing going.

Except . . . I do a bad thing.

I didn't mean to. I reveal a trick. I open a box before I should. The whole inside shows. I did it because I got hurt.

Our father makes it a joke the way he does when things happen that aren't supposed to. I see it does make a difference in how the audience feels. I have blood dripping down my leg, but I know the show must go on. I've gone on with a bad stomachache. Once I threw up every time I went backstage, but I knew I had to come back and go on, and not only that, I had to smile. That's what you have to do.

Those men made all sorts of jokes and said bad words, even though there were ladies present. But our father, even then, got everything back on track.

I lose my appetite for supper. Something's going to happen. I can see it in the way our father walks. Or maybe it's my own guilty conscience that makes him seem so scary. Except I didn't do it on purpose. I wasn't ready. I got scared. With reason. I have a cut to prove it. And maybe it was even his fault. Maybe he was too fast.

But "No excuses" is his favorite thing to say. When I grow up, I'm going let people have excuses.

"I've told you over and over, it's not for the likes of them to know."

"So I'm supposed to just lie there and lose half my leg?"

"It didn't come close to that and you know it."

"What do you call this, catsup?"

And then he does what he always does, twists my arm
up behind me, but this time . . .

I hear it crack. He's done it again. He hears it, too. He
gets an odd look on his face.

It really, really hurts.

Rosie sees everything. She's the one who yells the loud-
est yell. She runs out and starts pounding on our father.
Yelling and pounding. Next to our father she looks smaller
than ever.

Our father starts to laugh. He actually falls down
laughing—sits back on his fat hind end and laughs and
can't stop, and Rosie keeps pounding on him. Of course it's
not doing anything to hurt him.

Here comes Aunt Tilly, and I think, Now our father
will get it, but first she just stands and looks, at me then at
Rosie, then me and then Rosie again, and then she—even
she—starts to laugh. I guess it is funny, Rosie, pounding
away, yelling and kicking as hard as she can and not getting
anywhere. But here I am, trying to hang on to my broken
arm and nobody cares. Except Rosie.

And except Jocelyn. She comes right to me without
stopping to think or laugh. She forgot to put down her
knitting and the needles are falling out and the knitting is
unraveling. First she's afraid to touch me for fear she'll hurt
me. She reaches for my shoulder, but then puts her hand on
my head.

Finally Aunt Tilly pulls Rosie away and hugs her tight so she can't punch anymore, but she waited until she had herself a good laugh.

And here comes Mister Boots, looking like he doesn't know what to do.

And then I throw up, and then Boots gives a big whinny, sort of like that first time when he told me he was a horse only more so, lifts his head up and back, and starts so high . . . It's a kind of scream. You wouldn't think a horse could do that, nor a human being either.

That stops everybody. We're all posed, as if some big god said, "Silence!"

How can there be any doubt now about what Boots is? Except I'll bet nobody believes their ears. They'll all think: Did I really hear that? Then they'll think: I guess not. I couldn't have. I'll just wait until it happens again to see if it really did.

I get out of a whipping, except this is worse. Maybe worse—depending. It's an adventure because I get hauled off to the doctor in the big town—hauled off by Mister Boots and Jocelyn in a borrowed car. Our father disappears before they even find the car for me. (He never likes to be around throw-up. Besides, Mister Boots, as a horse, always did scare him. After that whinny, he'll wonder things.)

Before we go, Mister Boots binds my arm up tight to my body. He's good at that. He can sense how things feel a lot better than anybody I ever knew. He talks to me all the way through, making me think of other things.

Jocelyn drives. She's not good at it, and she doesn't like to (it's kind of jerky at first), but she always comes through when things are important. All the way to town, I don't even try not to cry. I tell Jocelyn I'm sorry but I can't help it, and she says it's all right, and I should do it as much as I want, so I do.

And then I tell her I'm even sorrier but I have to throw up again, and she says that's all right. Seems to be, when you break your arm, everything you do is suddenly all right.

At the hospital I get called a brave boy by the doctor, and told that most seven-year-olds aren't this brave. "How about girls?" I say. But the doctor just tousles my hair, and says, "Don't you worry about girls. Not yet."

But I really wanted to know.

The doctor says my arm isn't ever going to be the same, but it wasn't the same before, anyway.

I get to have a cast and I get pain pills that make me woozy. I get to have a maple walnut ice-cream cone. We get to stay all night in little cabins outside of town that are no bigger than our biggest tent. There's hardly room for the double bed and the cot. There are nice pictures all over the walls. Jocelyn says they were cut out of the *Saturday Evening Post*. I ask if we can do that someday if we ever settle down, and if we ever can afford a magazine. She says, "Don't be silly. Of course we can."

Boots and my sister register as Mr. and Mrs. Blue. I could hardly believe it considering how my sister said she wouldn't ever do anything to make Boots a real person on paper.

We don't have pajamas or anything, so I sleep in my underwear the way I used to do back before everything began to happen.

After we get back, nobody says one single word about Boots's whinny, so it's just as I thought. Or maybe it's embarrassing, like something you're not supposed to mention—a human being screaming a whinny out like that in public.

While we were gone, Rosie and Aunt Tilly went down to the little town we'd been to before and Aunt Tilly got Rosie two dolls. I'd have thought of that myself, but dolls always seemed too dangerous. Even Aunt Tilly never did dare get one for me, but she told Rosie one of these is really for me and which did she want? But Rosie said she told Aunt Tilly, since I'm the one with a broken arm, I should get first choice, but I knew Rosie would want the yellow-haired, blue-eyed one with ringlets, and I didn't want that one, anyway. She was too girlish. I may want to be what I really am, but there are limits.

I guess our father has kind of the same idea: I mean about giving me things in exchange for a broken arm. He sends a big package that is full of smaller packages. I get excited in spite of myself, though, since it's from our father, I ought to know better. Rosie and I open them alternating and as slowly as we can. We want to make the mystery of it last as long as possible. I know the mystery is going to be a lot better than the reality. I suppose that's how magic is, too—much better not to know. Which is exactly why I have a broken arm.

Rosie likes the presents more than I do. For her they're unusual, but I'm sick and tired of always getting things like this. First I open a toy fire engine, and then Rosie opens a soldier suit my size (which is Rosie's size, too). She says, "Please, please, please, please, can I have it, pleeeeease?"

"Of course, yes, and good riddance."

And another thing, more yarn. That must have been hard for him to give.

Then a big bag of pecans and a jar of honey and some oranges. Things he thinks are good for me.

Aunt Tilly says, "What if it was a couple of steaks to grill? Now that I would even cook myself."

Mostly we keep having stew, served on top of crackers. If you're rich enough for bacon, that goes in, and cheese, too, and most anything else. We're about rich enough for cabbage and corn and potatoes.

I've a good mind to go buy a steak for Aunt Tilly myself, but how would I explain how I got it? No matter what I said, everybody would think I stole it.

But we have to get out of here just like all the ordinary people. We start packing. I help even though I'm in a cast and my sling. I need to pack all my secret things, and I need to do it by myself.

When we sit around our campfire, we talk about where we should go, like maybe home to our house, but Aunt Tilly says our father will be back. She says whatever we decide to do, he'll change it no matter what it is, so we should just pack and not make plans.

He comes exactly on the next to last day, with a car and a wagon and plans for a performance just outside Los Angeles.

He comes at suppertime, but he won't eat our stew. He's smoking a cigar as usual, and then he gives us one of his lectures, so he must be feeling better now that he has a job lined up. The lecture is mostly to me.

It's dark when he comes. The days are getting shorter, and it's cooler. We have a big fire, and Mister Boots propped logs up behind it, slanty-wise, nice and neat, to throw the heat out toward us. Rosie and I sit next to each other like we always do. Our father stands on the far side, hands behind his back, looking even more like a devil than usual. The mustache and the little nothing of a goatee . . . Everything very neat. The red glow of the fire on his face reflecting red. Even his white shirt looks red.

It turns out I'm not out of the new show just because of a mere broken arm. I have a duty to my public to make an appearance even if I can't perform my usual tricks. Then he tells me, "You broke your arm in a fall from our trotter. That's how it happened."

We don't even *have* Houdie anymore.

I hear my sister gasp.

He says it again slowly and louder. "From. Our. Horse. You landed on your elbow."

He looks as if he believes it himself. I'm beginning to think he'll never believe anything that's true. I'll get breasts—maybe even big ones—I'll look like Aunt Tilly, and he'll still be calling me "Boy."

"Just go out and take a bow and do something simple. We'll do the cane duet. You can do a dove one-handed and a few scarves. You can pull them out of your cast. They'll go for that."

"When did you ever let me ride Houdie?"

"I hardly let myself ride him; you know that."

"How could I know that when you rode him all over the place back home? Besides, he's sold."

"That horse shouldn't be ridden at all, only by experts."

"Mister Boots is an expert."

"Your Mister Boots . . . He's hardly good for shoveling you-know-what."

We're all looking into the fire. We're all not saying

anything. Something has happened to us, which doesn't count our father. We work together like horses hitched to the same coach. Well, better than that, because some horses let other horses do most of the work. And here, Rosie appears with us and pulls with us, and we all pull together with her, too.

Next morning we're almost ready to leave. Mister Boots is about to take the garbage to the dumping spot. Big paper bags of it. (He always does the garbage jobs. He'll do all the messiest things. He doesn't want anybody else to have to do it, least of all Jocelyn.) Aunt Tilly is carrying packages to the wagon. I help take things that only need one good arm.

Our father is packing the wagon because he's the absolutely only one who, as he keeps saying, can do it properly. He keeps telling us, "For heaven's sake hold steady, for heaven's sake use your noggin, and hurry up; we have to get down south so we can unload while it's still daylight."

If he wasn't here we'd be just as fast—maybe faster—and I'll bet we'd all be humming.

The fire is still hot and the coffeepot is still propped on a stone near it for everybody's one last drink. (Except for me; I'm still not allowed coffee.) Jocelyn is sweeping the last tent. It's down, and she's sweeping the top of it before folding it up. She makes a funny face at Boots, and he waves and drops the garbage bags. (As a human being he's always so clumsy!) The garbage spills out of both of them. When our father sees that, he punches the railing of the wagon and then tosses his turban way, way out—I can't believe it—it knocks over the coffeepot and lands right in the fire.

"That's it!" he says. He jumps off the back of the wagon and heads right for Boots. Boots is leaning over, up to his elbows in garbage, trying to get it back together. Our father gives him a kick in the behind that knocks him right into the mess.

Talk about "That's it!" I'm tired of all this myself: tired of our father and tired of moving around from one place to another all the time and tired of having a broken arm and tired of not having any horses to ride and tired of me and Mister Boots always getting the brunt of everything.

I bellow out—my stage voice, but no words. A big, just plain bellow.

All right, this really is it.

By now I know better than to try and shout, "I'm a girl, I'm a girl." Nobody will pay attention, and our father will say, "Don't be sassy."

It's not so easy with a cast, but I take off all my clothes.

It doesn't take him—not half a minute—to realize. So fast I think he must have suspected.

He comes to our baggage, fat-man fast. . . .

Like I dreamed it before. And like a dream. The sound of the hippopotamus. Which I don't know what that is, but this is it. Fire crackling. The sword box burning, and the box where I disappear, even the swords and the saw, into the fire. Boxes with our clothes . . . gasping . . . sputtering . . . our father . . . making this hippopotamus noise.

I have my treasures packed up in my pockets, but my knickers are down around my feet now. I reach down to get the pistol, but our father pushes me away and reaches faster. He shakes my clothes and out comes everything. Money all over the place. The rubber bands that held it have broken. Money, in the air. Even in the fire. Which is bigger and bigger all the time.

And there's my pistol.

Everything is slowing down. I see the paint on the boxes fizzling, the red goes first and the gold after. I hear a raven sound a warning. I hear the stream. There's plenty of time. I pick up the pistol.

Except there isn't any time at all. I get off one shot. There's a thump and the ground spits where the bullet landed. Our father takes the gun as easy as could be and kicks me away like he did Boots. I'm going into the fire with everything else. I'm flat-out right in it.

Everybody's staring at the money flying by. Except Boots. It's Moonlight Blue, right into the fire, to me. To save me. A horse from . . . hellfire! Like that man said. Red and smoke and horse screams and the sound of the hippopotamus.

Our father, grinning like the crazy man, shoots. All the

rest of the shots, the four, into Moonlight Blue. And
Moonlight Blue topples over right in the middle of fire,
partly on me.

I think, as if looking back already: Once we had a horse.
A long time ago we had a horse who was a man. As sweet,
as sweet . . . as wet grass.

Sparks fly up. Blow! Way, way up all over. The money
flying up and away, too.

And here's my sister, hauling the collapsed tent, throwing it over both of us. I didn't know I was on fire, but I
guess I must have been. It's terrible under there, dusty and
smelly and suffocating. There are so many things in this life
you just have to do no matter what, and keep on doing.

I put my good arm around Moonlight Blue's neck.
"Don't die," I say. "Please don't die. I'll take you out to
where those wild mustangs are and let you go free. I don't
have any money anymore, but I'll find a way. Cross my
heart and hope to . . . Don't die."

I feel his soft, soft, velvety horse lips, as he blows
against my cheek. Like a sign. Like a kiss. What is there
ever in the whole wide world as soft as the lips of a horse?

And then he isn't blowing anymore.

I think about what Boots said about death, what I heard
him tell Jocelyn: "When I'm no longer able to hear the
tunes of your voice . . ."

And she said, "Why do you keep thinking about
death?"

"When we can, we twist and run, and when we can't . . . Human beings have little resignation about something we all have to do."

I hear people yelling and rushing around. I feel cold bumping down on Boots and me. The tent isn't leaking, but I feel the cold of the water through the canvas. Finally the tent gets pulled off, and I can breathe again.

chapter thirteen

Money isn't everything. Mister Boots said that all the time. But I think money really is something, the way all the people of the camping place ran around in circles that morning, yelling and trying to gather it up. There was a horse lying dead right there in front of them, and all they cared about was the money. Rosie, too. She was running around waving her arms and shouting, "Oh, no! Oh, no!"

Our father did the disappearing act, no mirrors, no boxes, no smoke. . . . Well, smoke. Nobody saw him go. The wagon and the car were still there. I guess he got too scared even to take the car, but after all, all he did was shoot a horse. Who cares about horses? Especially old lame ones? Of course he always thought that there was just a skinny, clumsy man who tripped over his own feet. When Jocelyn signed them in at the cabins as Mr. and Mrs. Blue, that's the only time there ever was a record that Boots existed.

❦

I'm finally out at our tree. I brought water like I always do. I didn't dare go before. I was scared that maybe Boots would be waiting there, naked and thirsty and glad to see me.

I lie down and look at the sky the horse way, through the dry yellow grass.

I don't want a world like this—Mother dead and Rosie's mother dead and Boots dead. The world never used to be like this back when nothing happened.

I can just hear Boots saying, "It's the world we were made for; that's why we like it so much. Taste of water, smell of hay . . . All ours."

But I'm thinking, No, it isn't. Not my world. I wasn't made for any of it.

"Mister Boots, you mustn't be gone! I especially need you now. I need you to tell me how to think about you not being here."

Odd to think I got myself and everybody else, too, into all this because I wanted to throw fire. That was my dream back then.

But it wasn't all me. Our father wanted me along. Knowing what I know about him now, I'll bet he would have kidnapped me if I hadn't wanted to come. And then Mister Boots and my sister would have followed, and everything would have happened just as it did. So I guess it's not all my fault.

Aunt Tilly says to look on the bright side. So I say to her, "Well, at least you're not dead yet." And she says, "For heaven's sake, the things that child thinks of."

"Well then, why do the songs you sing make us all so sad? Like 'Beautiful Dreamer.' There has to be a reasonable reason for singing all those songs. 'The Last Rose of Summer' and all. Are they looking on the bright side?"

"But look at all the good things. You have Rosie for another sister. You can be Roberta and not sneak around and steal dresses. You can be ten . . . well, eleven now. That's a nice number, too. Mister Boots would think so."

"He wouldn't."

"You know he would."

"I'd give all the good things away to have Mister Boots back."

"Honey, come sit on my lap now, even though you are eleven. Come. Don't think at all."

"Boots said, 'Think.'"

"He didn't mean *all* the time."

I guess there are a few good things. It's good when Aunt Tilly sings and plays the ukulele. And she's teaching me. She sings and plays the piano at the hotel in town every weekend and makes money.

Another good thing: I'm finally growing. We've been measuring. It's right there on the doorway.

Rosie and I get to go to the village school. I stick up for

her. I fight for her even though she's bigger than I am. It's as if I'm still thinking of myself as a boy.

We have a lot of secrets—new ones, little ones, and one great big one—but not any more about our ages or what sex we are.

And another good thing: the baby. Sometimes my sister holds her on her lap, "as foal or girl," just like Mister Boots would say. We expect, as a horse that is, she'll turn as light-colored as her father as she gets older. We all want her to be a flea-bit gray.

Moonlight Marilyn Blue.

She's the big secret, but I'm used to secrets.

She's especially a secret if our father ever comes back. Jocelyn doesn't want Marilyn to have a life like Boots's.

Our father would like her too much. She could make a lot of money and she'd look good on a poster. If he found out, I'll bet he wouldn't even care if she was a girl or not.

She looks kind of funny, but of course all new babies look funny. I know that much. She has Boots's big caramel-colored eyes and long head; fuzzy, black, baby foal hair. . . .

It'll be like I was. They won't dare send her to school for fear people will find out. With me it was that I wasn't a boy; with her it's different. They'll have to wait at least until she's old enough to keep herself a secret, so I'll teach her. She'll get to know every single thing I know.

It's good we have her. Jocelyn would feel too bad about Boots without Marilyn to care for.

Sometimes I think maybe I'd be even more of a triumph going onstage as a girl magician, wearing a scanty costume like Aunt Tilly used to wear. (If I ever get breasts.) My helper would be a man in a dress suit, top hat, and all—and a goatee. I'd make him curl up in boxes. I'd saw him in half and stick him full of swords. When I get to be a grown-up, I can do anything I want.

Right now I have to go to school and grow up a little more. Jocelyn says that's what Mister Boots would say, and he would.

But it seems like an awful long wait. People always tell me I'll change my mind when I get older. I hope I don't because being a magician is what I really, really, really want to do.

CAROL EMSHWILLER is the author of many acclaimed novels and story collections, including *Carmen Dog*, *The Start of the End of It All* (winner of the World Fantasy Award), *Report to the Men's Club and Other Stories*, *The Mount* (winner of the Philip K. Dick Award and a Nebula Award Finalist), and *I Live with You and You Don't Know It*. In the winter, she lives in New York City and teaches in the NYU Continuing Education program; in the summer, she lives in Bishop, California, between the Sierras and the Inyo White Mountains.

Her Web site is www.sfwa.org/members/emshwiller